'You're not t

Adam's blue eye
'You don't smoke or keep late nights. You do
sleep around. So what vices have you got, little
Tina Reynolds?'

Christina gritted her teeth. Little Tina
Reynolds? He made her sound like someone
who had just progressed out of dolls and easy-
to-read books.

'I don't like men who patronise,' she answered
calmly.

Dear Reader

There's nothing more wonderful than celebrating the end of winter, with an exciting collection of books to choose from! Mills & Boon will transport you to all corners of the world, including two enchanting Euromance destinations—sun-drenched, exotic Madeira contrasting with scenic evergreen Wales. Let the spring sunshine brighten up your day by reading our romances which are bursting with love and laughter! So why not treat yourself to many hours of happy reading?

The Editor

Cathy Williams is Trinidadian and was brought up on the twin islands of Trinidad and Tobago. She was awarded a scholarship to study in Britain, and came to Exeter University in 1975 to continue her studies into the great loves of her life: languages and literature. It was there that Cathy met her husband, Richard. Since they married Cathy has lived in England, originally in the Thames Valley but now in the Midlands. Cathy and Richard have two small daughters.

Recent titles by the same author:

TOO SCARED TO LOVE
BITTERSWEET LOVE

UNWILLING SURRENDER

BY
CATHY WILLIAMS

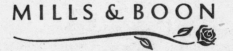

MILLS & BOON LIMITED
ETON HOUSE, 18-24 PARADISE ROAD
RICHMOND, SURREY TW9 1SR

*First published in Great Britain 1994
by Mills & Boon Limited*

© Cathy Williams 1994

*Australian copyright 1994
Philippine copyright 1994
This edition 1994*

ISBN 0 263 78426 6

*Set in Times Roman 10 on 11½ pt.
01-9403-55131 C*

Made and printed in Great Britain

CHAPTER ONE

IT WAS two-thirty in the morning and the telephone was ringing. Right next to her bed. Sharp, insistent rings that demanded answering, and her immediate groggy thought was that some catastrophe had occurred. Something awful that couldn't wait until a more civilised hour. After all, what voice at the end of a telephone at two-thirty in the morning was going to be the bearer of good tidings?

For a split-second she was tempted to let the damn thing ring, to let the bad news wait until morning, but she couldn't. It wasn't in her nature. She had never had much success in dodging reality and she wasn't about to achieve it now.

She reluctantly lifted the receiver and waited for the person on the other end to speak. Which he did.

'I knew you were there.' That dark, velvety voice which could charm the birds off the trees was cold and abrupt and Christina felt her head thicken with a sudden, overwhelming tension, even though she told herself that that was silly. She was a grown woman of twenty-three and she had nothing to fear from Adam Palmer.

But old habits died hard. Ever since she was a child, he had been able to fill her with a similar sickening nervousness.

'What do you want?' she asked, knowing immediately why he had called and forestalling his inevitable question. 'Have you any idea what time it is?' Her head felt as clear as a bell, her mind alert and already in a position of self-defence.

5

'I know exactly what the time is,' he returned dismissively, 'and, just in case you're waiting for an apology for my phoning you at this hour, there won't be one forthcoming. So don't hold your breath.'

Oh, charming, she thought angrily. Has it occurred to you that I might not exactly relish being dragged out of sleep at this ungodly hour?

She had a mental image of him. Tall, strikingly handsome and frighteningly clever. A man who had probably never suffered even the most fleeting attack of self-consciousness in his entire life. She doubted that he had even given a second's thought to the hour of his phone call.

She sat up straighter in her bed, her body stiff even though she was alone in the bedroom.

'You could have waited until morning,' she began on an indrawn breath, hanging on to some semblance of politeness while her mind conjured up satisfying pictures of him falling down a couple of flights of stairs, or finding himself lost in the middle of a desert somewhere with no help in sight. 'You may think nothing of being up at this hour, but some of us happen to lead more orthodox lives.'

'Cocoa at nine and then bed by nine-thirty, Tina?' There was lazy mockery in his voice, and it sent the blood rushing to her head.

How wonderful to have been able to think of some bitingly acid retort, but as usual on these occasions her mind went blank.

She made a little strangled sound down the line and then took a deep breath, counting to ten. It was unwise to enter into any sort of argument with Adam Palmer, because he invariably won. In fact, it was unwise to let yourself become in the slightest bit ruffled by anything he had to say.

'Yes,' she said calmly, 'and very enjoyable it is too, except when I get bothered by phone calls at this hour in the morning.'

'What an exciting little girl you are,' he remarked, in the same mocking voice, and she could have screamed. 'But fascinating though your personal life is, you know my reason for calling you. Where the hell is my sister?'

'I have no idea.'

'And now that you've got that little lie off your chest, why don't you tell me the truth? Where is she?'

She should have prepared some suitable lie. She had known as soon as Fiona flew the nest that her brother would come barging along for a few answers. After all, she was Fiona's closest friend. But lying didn't come easy to Christina. She was a placid, self-controlled girl who found that the wheels of life moved far more smoothly without intrigue.

'I can't tell you that,' she said into the waiting silence, and she heard the furious intake of breath down the other end. 'Fiona made me promise not to reveal her whereabouts.'

'Oh, she did, did she?'

'She's not a child any longer, Adam,' she continued hastily, because it didn't take a genius to realise that his rage was climbing a few degrees higher with every word she spoke. 'She's twenty-two now. She can vote, she can go to pubs, she can even get married if she wants to.'

'So that's what she's up to, is it?' he bellowed down the line, and Christina held the phone a little way back from her ear. 'Marriage? To that...that...'

'You'll get high blood-pressure if you don't relax,' she said with a weak attempt to defuse the situation, which was utterly futile.

'You'll damn well get high blood-pressure in a minute,' he roared. 'I'm on my way over.'

She heard the slam of the receiver and then that dead dialling tone and she looked at the phone with mounting horror.

On his way over? To her flat? Now? The prospect of Adam swooping down at her in a thunderous rage and demanding answers out of her made her tremble with apprehension. It had been bad enough merely hearing his voice down the receiver.

She thought of him in his Jaguar screeching over and her body was galvanised into action. Very quickly, she washed her face, combed her hair sensibly away from her face, and stuck on a pair of jeans and a jumper, feeling very odd being suddenly fully clothed when less than half an hour ago she was cocooned under a layer of blankets, sound asleep.

Fiona, she thought, this is all your fault. Why did you have to involve me in your wretched schemes?

But she really wasn't cross with her friend. She had known her as long as she had known Adam, which was getting on for fifteen years, and she had long ago accepted her for what she was—an adorable, impulsive creature, who sailed through life blithely ignoring anything that remotely resembled cares or worries.

That, perhaps, had been the essence of their friendship, the reason why it had survived intact for so long. Opposites attracted, and Christina knew that she was exactly the opposite of her friend: composed where Fiona was apt to dramatise, controlled, level-headed, practical.

They even looked completely different. Fiona was small and intensely pretty, with raven-black hair like her brother, and the same vivid blue eyes. She had spent her life captivating men. It was the thing, she often told Christina, that she did best.

She, Christina, on the other hand, was tall and slender, without the curves that men seemed to go for. Her hair was an unremarkable brown, falling straight to her shoulders. She had long ago abandoned any attempt to make it appear more interesting than in fact it was. Her eyes, also brown, were usually serene. Only close observation revealed them to be what she in fact herself was, namely astute and humorous.

She glimpsed her reflection in the mirror and grimaced. She was plain. There was no denying that. It was one of those inescapable facts of life, like the sun rising every morning. She accepted it and in fact she was often thankful for it, because great beauty often brought great problems, whereas she could continue, for the most part, on her merry way, without her life being disturbed overmuch. She was never a threat to other women, and consequently had quite a few girlfriends, men enjoyed her company without any of that macho need to make a pass and, all in all, life was calm and enjoyable.

Only Adam Palmer had ever made her acutely aware of her lack of looks.

Not that he was cruel or derisory. Maybe it was because his own life was so crammed with gorgeous women that she immediately felt, in his presence, as if she was being given the once-over and found wanting.

She waited gloomily on the sofa in the lounge for his appearance, perched on the edge of the chair like a patient waiting for the dentist to summon.

He wouldn't be long, she knew that. They both lived in London, albeit in wildly different areas. Her flat was a modest two-bedroomed place in Clapham. His house was a massive affair in north London, in an area where the profusion of trees could actually make you forget that you weren't in suburbia.

He had inherited it on his parents' death seven years previously, and he had lived there ever since with Fiona, looking after his sister with a fierce protectiveness which had often made Christina smile, but which Fiona, admittedly, had sometimes found stifling and exasperating.

She heard his car before the doorbell went. There was a squeal of tyres, then three sharp buzzes on the doorbell.

Christina resignedly pressed the button to open the main door in the lobby, and unlocked her own front door.

Then she waited on the sofa, hearing his footsteps mounting the stairs, and the rap on the front door, which was pushed open before she had finished telling him to come in.

He brought the cold air of winter with him. It clung to the black coat and the temperature in the room seemed to drop a few degrees. Christina reluctantly found her eyes drawn to him, looking at him and feeling as overawed and as taken aback as if she had never seen him in her life before.

Because every time she saw him she realised that she had forgotten just how tall and commanding his presence was. It filled the flat, giving off a vibrating, impatient energy that made you think of some caged jungle animal.

'Would you like some coffee?' she asked, standing up and watching him as he removed his coat and then sank on to one of the chairs, for all the world as though he were an invited guest.

'Have you got anything stronger?' he asked, fixing her with those amazing blue eyes of his. 'Whisky? Gin?'

Christina's lips tightened a fraction. Trust him, she thought. In a minute he'll be mentioning that he feels a bit peckish and could I fix him a little something to eat.

'There might be some wine in the fridge,' she said with an edge to her voice that she hoped would leave him in no doubt that he was unwanted in her flat. 'I don't normally keep a supply of hard liquor in the flat.'

'Very pointed,' Adam observed, running his eyes over her in a way that made her think that he probably did that automatically every time he was with a woman, whatever her age or appearance. 'No, forget the wine. I'll have a cup of coffee, please, black and very sweet.' He rubbed his fingers over his eyes. 'God, I'm exhausted,' he said. 'Up at six this morning, back home at two-thirty, only to be confronted with some damn note from that sister of mine informing me that she's gone, God knows where.'

'What a stressful life you lead,' Christina said without sympathy.

Back at two-thirty in the morning? Her heart was not bleeding. Chances were high that he had been out enjoying himself in the company of one of his entourage of glamorous adorers. Tired he might be, but only because he had no doubt been burning the candle at both ends.

She stalked into the kitchen and banged about in the cupboards, hoping that all the noise would end up giving him a thumping headache, and finally emerged ten minutes later with two mugs of coffee.

'You knew about this, didn't you?' he asked as soon as she had handed him his coffee.

Christina didn't reply immediately. She walked across to the sofa and sat down, tucking her long legs under her and taking a tentative sip from her mug.

Adam gave an impatient click of his tongue. 'Well?' he demanded, raking his fingers through his black hair in a frustrated, angry gesture. 'Don't just sit there. Answer me! You knew all about my sister and her harebrained plans, didn't you?'

Christina felt some of her calm evaporating. It had always been the same with him. She could remember being roused to rage in her early teens, stamping her feet, while he looked on, quite satisfied with his achievement, thinking that he could pour oil on troubled waters with the offer of tea in a café somewhere.

She couldn't stamp her feet now, but she still felt like doing it.

'You're in my flat now,' she said defensively, 'and I would appreciate it if you don't try to bully me into answering your questions.'

Adam frowned. 'Me? Bully? I have no idea what you're talking about. You always were a little over-sensitive, Tina.'

With remarkable restraint, she let that one go.

'I don't know why you bothered to come over here,' she said, fighting to hang on to her self-control. 'I'm not going to tell you anything more than I already have.'

'Dammit, Tina! Why are you protecting her? I only want to find out her whereabouts so that I know she's safe.'

'She's safe. Trust me.'

'I'd rather not. Where is she?'

He had sat forward a little and she could feel his personality enfolding her so that it was a struggle to think clearly.

The man was hypnotic. Those eyes could prise out the most guarded of secrets. He would look you straight in the face, forcing you to fall under the spell of his powerful, persuasive personality, and slowly but surely he would end up finding out exactly what he wanted.

Little wonder women were forever tripping over themselves in their haste to grab a little bit of him, to try their luck at netting the biggest fish in the sea.

But she wasn't one of his women. She had also known him long enough to see right through those tactics.

She stared back at him and repeated that her friend's whereabouts were strictly confidential.

'If she had wanted you to know, she would have told you in her note,' Christina pointed out with irrefutable logic, and he glared at her furiously.

'Stop trying to be clever with me! You know she wouldn't let on to me what her plans were. For some reason she seems to think that I'm a bit over-protective.' He transferred his glare to the mug of coffee, as if it had suddenly become responsible for his irritating situation, and Christina smiled.

Sometimes the set of his features reminded her of when he was much younger, and right now was one of those times. He had always been as stubborn as they came.

He looked up and caught her smiling and said angrily, 'I'm glad you find the whole thing so amusing. You might not be quite so amused if Fiona lands herself in a spot of trouble. You know what she's like just as well as I do. She has her head in the clouds. She goes through life thinking that nothing untoward could possibly happen to her, and one of these days that attitude is going to get her into a lot of trouble. The world isn't ready to cope with my sister's brand of naïveté.'

Christina knew that what he was saying was true. She also knew that trying to keep Fiona under lock and key was not the way to overcome any potential problems.

The truth of the matter was that Adam Palmer found his inability to restrain his sister frustrating. Unlike everything and everyone else in life, she refused to respond to his persuasion. Oh, she listened well enough, and nodded her head in all the right places, but then she proceeded to do just precisely as she wanted.

'You can't fight all her battles for her,' Christina said eventually. 'She has to learn from her own mistakes. Trying to run her life for her is just going to make her resent you.'

'Is that what she told you? That she resents me?'

Christina sighed heavily. They were getting precisely nowhere and she was feeling very tired.

'More or less,' she hedged, and Adam stood up and walked across to her.

'And I suppose you agree?' He leant over her, gripping the back of the sofa on either side of her so that she was trapped by him.

She found her breath coming in small, quick gasps.

'She has to make her own mistakes,' she stammered, confused by his proximity and wishing that he would remove himself to some other, safer, part of the room. Or, better still, out of her flat altogether.

'And you think that that includes marrying Simon West? That snivelling leech who's only attracted to her because of her money? Should I stand back and watch her make that ultimate mistake without trying to do anything about it?'

He was still leaning over her, and she found that her thought processes seemed to have seized up.

The sensation brought back vivid and unwelcome memories of when she was a teenager, and hopelessly infatuated with him. Then, she had experienced that same dizzy, disorientated feeling whenever he was around. It would have faded away of its own accord, she was certain of that, despite the power that he had held over her, but time and adulthood had not been allowed to take their course. He had spotted the intensity of her private feelings with the shrewd perceptiveness of the born predator and he had laughed them off. Young and tactless, he had found her infatuation amusing, and that had left a sharp tang of bitterness in her mouth.

But that was a long time ago. She had recovered from that inconvenient passing fever. She had moved on with her life.

'He may not be as bad as he seems,' Christina muttered feebly, thinking of Fiona's latest boyfriend with distaste. She had met him a few times, and each time some new feature of his personality had further reduced her impression of him. She could understand Adam's concern.

He swung around from her and began prowling through the room, absent-mindedly looking at the pictures on the walls, the ornaments on the tables.

'He's as bad as he seems,' he said finally, 'and worse. How could you let her run off with him? You're supposed to be her friend.'

Stung, Christina's head snapped up.

'I'm not her keeper!' she bit out angrily. 'Of course I didn't encourage her in her plans to go to...in her plans. I tried to talk her out of it, but when Fiona decides to dig her heels in she does so with a vengeance. She wouldn't listen to a word I was saying. And in the end, it's her life.'

Adam stared at her as if she were some foreign species of animal. And she knew why. He was accustomed to having his orders obeyed. He had come to expect it. All this talk about freedom of choice was irritating for him, because he knew what was right for his sister and he could not understand why she failed to see his point of view.

What made matters worse, Christina thought, was that the damned man *was* always right.

'Are you going to tell me where she's gone?' he asked softly, moving to sit alongside her on the sofa.

She shuffled inconspicuously away from him so that she was pressed against the armrest and eyed him drily. 'You don't give up, do you? You're like a dog with a bone.'

For the first time since he had barged his way into her flat, his features relaxed into a smile, a coaxing, charming smile which she had observed on his face before—when he had been in the company of a beautiful woman. It had always amazed her that none of these women could see through it to the single-minded, relentless man underneath, the one who had taken his father's ailing company and turned it around in a matter of months, the one with the reputation in business circles of being a force to be reckoned with.

He must be a very good actor, she decided, if he could sublimate all those characteristics in his relationships with women.

Was he hoping now that he could pull that smile on her and coax her around to his way of thinking?

Did he really think that she was as empty-headed and as eager to be pleased as the women he chose to be associated with?

'You know me, Tina.' He smiled again and she ignored it.

'Unfortunately.'

'You don't mean that. Next to my sister, you're my longest-standing female friend.'

Lucky old me, she thought. He makes me sound like a piece of furniture that's stood in the same place for a thousand years.

'I shouldn't be too proud of that fact if I were you,' she muttered, thinking that he would not hear her, but of course he had. His eyes narrowed, even though the smile was still playing on his lips.

'Meaning?'

'Why boast about the fact that you shed women with appalling regularity?'

'Don't you start preaching to me!' He scowled at her and she smiled back at him.

Had Fiona been telling him the same thing? she wondered. Normally she did not stand up to him. Maybe she was developing a little bit of fighting spirit. Christina hoped so. The world, as far as she could see, was altogether too short of people who were prepared to give Adam Palmer a piece of their mind.

Money bred an unhealthy awe in people, and he was wealthy enough to have inspired this kind of awe for a number of years. Combine that wealth with a brilliant, restless intellect and good looks, and the combination was fatal.

'Well, you do have a certain reputation,' she murmured in a honeyed voice.

'Not one that I've ever courted.'

'You'll have to excuse me if I don't agree.'

'Will I?' He leaned back and surveyed her from under thick black lashes. 'I don't know how you can be an authority on my love-life when you've never been a part of it.'

Christina felt her cheeks go pink, but her composure remained firmly in place. She looked at him in silence, wondering how on earth she had ever had a crush on this man.

'In fact,' he said with a certain amount of lazy good humour, 'have you ever been an authority on anyone's love-life? I've known you all these years, yet you've never changed from being the cool little creature who always studied hard at school and always, always had her head screwed firmly on the right way.'

Christina could have thrown the lamp at him. Aiming straight for his head. Who did he think he was with his snide insinuations and thinly disguised insults?

'There's nothing wrong with that,' she replied evenly, but some of the tranquillity of her expression had evaporated.

'Not terribly exciting, though, is it?'

'Please, spare me your observations on what makes an exciting life. If exciting means bed-hopping the way that you do, then you're welcome to it.'

She heard her voice sounding acid and prim and she could have kicked herself.

His blue eyes had taken on a distinctly wicked gleam at that. Wasn't he tired? He had said earlier on that he was, but there was nothing tired about the man sitting next to her now. He looked invigorated, ready for a few hours of discussion, probably on her love-life, or lack of it, which he seemed to find highly entertaining. Maybe this was his sly way of extracting his pound of flesh for her silence over Fiona's whereabouts.

'What a damning statement,' he said. 'Bed-hopping? You have a very vivid imagination. I may have slept with a few women in my time, but I certainly don't make a habit of jumping in and out of beds on a routine basis. Any chance of another cup of coffee?' He held out his mug and Christina looked at it scathingly.

'No chance whatsoever. I'm tired and it's time that you left. I have no intention of telling you where Fiona's gone, so you might as well forget it, Adam.'

His lips thinned.

'I'll do nothing of the sort. If you don't tell me what I want to know, I'll personally make sure that Simon West pays for any mistakes that my sister's made.'

'How do you intend to do that?' Christina asked apprehensively. She had no doubt that he could and would do precisely as he had threatened. He certainly pulled enough strings, had enough power in the right circles to ensure that his threats weren't hollow ones.

'He's an actor, isn't he?'

She nodded without saying anything.

'A very precarious position, wouldn't you agree?'

She nodded again and felt like a mouse that had strayed into a trap and was waiting for it to clamp shut.

'I've been on the look-out for a theatre company to buy. There could be a lot of money in that. I've been meaning to broaden my interests in the field of the arts for quite some time now.' He allowed a little silence to fall between them. 'It's a tight community, the artistic community. One word about someone can spread faster than a bush fire.' He turned the mug over in his hands, inspecting it.

'You wouldn't ruin his career,' Christina whispered, horrified. 'You couldn't.'

'I'll do what I can to protect my sister.' He slammed the mug down on to the coffee-table, making her jump.

He had put her in an impossible situation. Keep quiet and risk watching Simon West's career, such as it was, bite the dust. Tell all and betray her friend's confidence.

Simon might be everything that Adam had said he was. Certainly, from what she had seen, he was vain, egotistic and irritatingly convinced that the world was somehow a better place with him in it. But she could not stand aside and let Adam do his worst.

'All right,' she said wearily. 'They're using that cottage in Scotland. The one your parents owned.'

'That?' Adam gave her a long, hard look and then began to laugh. 'Well, I can't see romance blossoming in that run-down place, can you? Especially in weather like this. West hardly strikes me as the sort of man who knows how to survive without central heating and all mod cons.'

'Fiona said that they needed privacy.'

'She gets privacy. In fact she has all the room she needs.'

'Very little, when you're under the same roof,' Christina said under her breath, and he frowned.

'Well, I shall have to go up there and try and talk some sense into her. Just in case she's contemplating doing something crazy.' He stood up and immediately the lounge seemed to shrink in size.

'Like what?' Christina asked, momentarily distracted by the sheer power of his presence.

'Like marrying the half-wit.' He snatched up his coat and began putting it on. Black and thick, it gave him the air of a raffish highwayman, not that he seemed aware of the impression he made. He was frowning, thinking.

'Wouldn't they need a licence or something?' Christina asked, anxious now. 'Besides, Fiona has more sense than that.' But her voice was even more dubious.

'Who knows how long they've been planning this little jaunt?' He looked at her narrowly, and she shook her head in answer to his unspoken question.

'I, for one, did not,' she denied vehemently. 'Fiona dropped this on me like a bombshell yesterday.'

He was staring at her, as if trying to work something out in his mind, and it made her uneasy. Nothing was ever straightforward with Adam Palmer. She rose to her feet and walked across to the door, her hand resting lightly on the handle.

He had got what he wanted, she thought. She could have saved herself a lot of trouble merely by recognising from the very start that he was going to get the information out of her, and by telling him what he wanted to know without bothering to beat about the bush.

But he had always brought out the argumentative side in her. Even when she had been madly infatuated with him, when she used to follow him with her eyes every time she saw him, she had still never been submissive enough to listen to what he had to say without responding.

He moved across to the door to stand by her, looking down at her with a calculating little gleam in his eyes.

'Busy right now?' he asked, and she stared into his blue eyes, surprised and taken aback by his sudden digression.

'Quite busy, yes,' she said warily. 'Why?'

He shrugged. 'Merely being polite. After all, we've hardly exchanged pleasantries since I got here.'

'I don't remember a time when that bothered you particularly,' Christina commented matter-of-factly.

He raised one brow, but she knew that he really couldn't care less what she thought of him. He liked her well enough; time, after all, did bring a certain unsought familiarity into any relationship. But as far as he was concerned she existed on his periphery. His sister's friend. The plain little girl who had grown into a quite ordinary-looking young woman. He had never looked twice at her and he never would, and so he had nothing to prove with her. He didn't even have to pretend to care what she thought about him.

'What interesting jobs have you got lined up? Fiona keeps me well informed about your fascinating line of work.'

'Does she?' Christina asked politely, thinking that he sounded anything but fascinated.

'What was your last project? Photographing a member of royalty for a magazine cover?'

Christina nodded and wondered where this line of questioning was leading.

'Must be very convenient, freelancing,' he murmured, looking at her sideways. 'I sometimes wish I had that sort of luxury.'

'What? And give up the stress of the concrete jungle?' she asked sarcastically. 'I don't believe that for one minute, Adam.'

He laughed softly. 'No, perhaps you're right,' he murmured. 'Still, you work to your own timetable, don't you?'

'Not really.'

He ignored that. 'Which is particularly convenient right at this moment, because I want you to come with me to Scotland to fetch my sister.'

CHAPTER TWO

'YOU want what?' Christina stared at him as though he had gone completely mad and he stared back at her with an insufferable look of patience on his face.

'I want you to come with me to Scotland,' he repeated, very slowly, 'to fetch my sister. You've already agreed that she was crazy to have just vanished with that fool of a boy. Who knows where it will lead? And if she makes the mistake of marrying him, it'll be over my dead body. So naturally I have to prevent that from happening at all costs.'

'Oh, naturally,' Christina spluttered angrily. 'You go right ahead and do what you feel you have to do, but please don't include me in your plans.'

She opened the front door and a cold blast of air wafted in.

Her flat did not lead directly out to the street, but rather on to a small landing shared by her neighbour's adjacent flat. Even so, it was cold outside.

He pushed the door shut and leant against it, his arms folded.

'You have to come, Tina, you're her friend. Supposedly.'

She gave him a long, withering look. She hoped it spoke volumes, because she didn't trust her vocabulary to cover precisely what she wanted to say on the subject, which was a good deal.

'Don't you dare use that sort of blackmail on me,' she said emphatically. 'You might be able to get your way with most people, over most things, but not with me and definitely not on this matter!'

There, she thought, take that.

But instead of moving out of her way, instead of acknowledging defeat, he continued to look at her, his face grim. He wasn't playing any games when it came to this. She could see that. Ever since his parents had died, he had taken care of his sister zealously. Despite her age, he considered her his responsibility, probably until she settled down and married someone in whom he could safely entrust her well-being.

As far as he was concerned, Fiona was in danger of committing the biggest mistake of her short life and he was not going to stand around without doing something about it.

Christina could follow that line of thought, even though she wasn't quite sure whether she agreed with it or not.

However, as far as she was concerned, coercing her into some kind of confrontation with his sister was out of the question.

She was not about to start taking sides with anyone, because she would have hated it if she had been in Fiona's situation. Hardly likely, she acknowledged honestly, since highly unsuitable men weren't attracted to her in the slightest, but that was not the point.

'I'm not leaving here until you agree to accompany me,' he said blandly enough, although his face was hard and determined. 'You know my sister as well as I do. She'll have a fit if I show up on the doorstep, playing big brother. But if she sees you, she might feel more inclined to listen to sense.'

'Alternatively, she might just slam the door in both our faces and tell us to mind our own damn business!'

'It's a risk we'll have to take.'

'Correction; it's a risk *you'll* have to take.'

She glared at him and he reached out and gripped her by her arm, pulling her towards him so that their faces were only inches apart.

'Now you listen to me,' he said with razor sharpness. 'You're coming with me whether you like it or not. You can just get down from that "you're entitled to do what you like in life" platform. This is Fiona and we're not talking about some casual little fling here. She's been seeing this boy for quite a while and she seems serious about him.'

'It might be mutual,' Christina interjected feebly, but she was on weak ground here, she knew that.

'We both know that that's not the case. God knows why my sister can't see the obvious, but that's irrelevant. The fact is, I don't want her doing anything she'd live to regret.' He took a deep breath and looked at her coldly. His fingers were still biting into her arm, and Christina gave a little tug, which he ignored. 'Have I told you that he was throwing out feelers as to how much money she stands to acquire on her twenty-fifth birthday?'

Christina gasped, appalled. 'No! Surely not!'

'Yes, that's right.'

'Did you mention that to Fiona?'

He gave a short, cynical laugh. 'Don't be ridiculous. That would have had the opposite effect.' He released her abruptly and she massaged her numb arm, trying to get the blood circulation back into action.

'You're probably right,' she agreed.

'Now do you still think that it's all right to let her get on with her own mistakes?'

'She's a grown woman,' Christina protested helplessly, but his revelation had taken the wind out of her sails and she knew that his sharp eyes had not missed that.

'She's got years of living to do before she can be called that,' he said bluntly, though his eyes were indulgent. 'She's always been as flighty as a butterfly, and I've always accepted that. But not this time. This boy is a nasty piece of work. He could ruin her life.'

There was a little silence between them while Christina digested all this.

She had not banked on any of this happening. Oh, she had known that he would contact her as soon as he had read Fiona's note, but she had been adamant that she would reveal nothing of her friend's whereabouts.

Not only had she failed miserably in that decision, but here she was, teetering on the brink of agreeing with him that yes, maybe chasing her up to that cottage in Scotland wasn't such a bad idea after all.

The man's powers of persuasion were limitless.

'Well?' he pressed. 'What's your decision?'

'I can't just rush off and leave my work commitments,' Christina said weakly, grasping at straws.

'You'll be gone two days at the outset. It's hardly going to kill any potential jobs you might have.'

He had a point, she thought with an inward sigh of resignation. February was not a good time for her, for some reason. There was enough work to keep her going, but nothing like the demand which she normally had for the remainder of the year.

'Not that that would stop you,' she muttered gloomily, but he was relaxed now, smiling even, though with no real humour.

He had succeeded in getting her where he wanted her, and if she could have she would have wiped that look of satisfaction off his clever face, but she couldn't.

'Now, now,' he soothed, 'you make me sound like a tyrant.'

'Do I?' She raised her large brown eyes to his. 'And that would be so far from the truth, wouldn't it?'

He laughed, a low chuckle that somehow managed to addle her.

'When you were much younger, I would have slapped you over your rear for that piece of cheek,' he said, still with that crooked smile.

'You always did have a way about you,' she said with asperity, but her face had gone pink at the thought of Adam Palmer's laying a hand on her, for whatever reason. 'When do you propose to leave for Scotland?' she asked, changing the subject, and he frowned, thinking about it.

'As soon as possible. We can take the shuttle out of Heathrow Airport to Glasgow and then drive to the cottage. Arduous, but it's the only way of getting there. I'll give you a call as soon as I find out the details. We can meet at the airport.'

'What about the weather?' This consideration had only just occurred to her, but there was no way that she was going to find herself stranded in that cottage, which she knew from old was in the middle of nowhere, alone with him. That was the sort of stuff that bred nightmares.

'What about it?'

'Snow?' she said patiently. 'Impassable roads? Stuck miles away from civilisation?'

'Dear me,' he murmured with an aggravating note of mockery in his voice, 'we can't have that, can we?'

'It's not a joke!' Christina snapped. 'I have no intention of being stuck up there with only you for company.' Her skin prickled at the mere thought of it.

No doubt there were hordes of women who would give their right arm to be in that situation. No doubt that was what was flashing through his mind even as he stood there, looking down at her with that annoying half-amused look on his face. But she was going to make it absolutely clear that she was not to be counted in that number.

She would listen to the weather reports and if there was any mention of snow—any mention of a passing flurry, for that matter—she would cancel that trip without giving it a second thought.

'There was a time,' he countered smoothly, 'when you would have found that thought quite appealing.'

She met his eyes and looked away in sudden confusion.

'And what is that supposed to mean?' she heard herself asking.

'Oh, you know what I mean, Tina. Remember that crush you had on me? You must have been all of what— fifteen? Sixteen? Sweet sixteen and never been kissed? I should have been flattered, but it was awkward, wasn't it?'

Christina's mouth went dry. She wanted the ground to open and swallow her up. Anything to spare her from this awful, nightmarish embarrassment washing over her.

'You must have——'

'Stop it!' she interrupted in a high voice. She took a deep breath, counted to ten, and when she next spoke she was relieved to hear that some of her self-control had returned. 'I was young. And stupid. Very stupid. Fortunately for me, I was cured of that little problem. So there's no point in dragging it up, is there? The fact of the matter is I'm not going unless the weather reports are favourable, and that's that.'

She couldn't quite bring herself to meet his eyes, so she stared at her fingers instead. A thousand things were running through her head, but really they all amounted to the same awful, vicious circle of memories that she had tried to put to the back of her mind. She had been so naïve. She had literally thrown herself at him and he had laughed with that sickening mixture of surprise and genuine amusement. 'You're a child,' he had told her but what he had meant was that she just didn't possess the easy charm and bold beauty of the women to whom he was already drawn.

What a picture she must have made, with her mousy brown hair and brown eyes, next to those blondes and brunettes and redheads who had adorned his parents' house with predictable regularity during the university holidays.

'Of course,' he said, 'I have no intention of getting stuck in ten-foot snowdrifts either. Not that your honour isn't safe with me, so you needn't fear anything on that score. You're Fiona's friend and...' He shrugged and the unspoken words hung in the air, their meaning crystal-clear. He found her physically unappealing, was what he was saying, so she could relax, but instead of reassuring her it brought tears of anger and humiliation to her eyes. It reminded her of how she had felt when her teenage crush had been ever so smilingly handed back to her.

'I'll call you.'

'Fine,' she said stiffly, looking at her watch. It was nearly five in the morning. He had been there much longer than she had thought. Hours. 'Now do you mind? I want to catch up on some sleep. As you do too, no doubt.' She hadn't meant to, but her voice implied that he needed the rest since he had spent the night doing God only knew what, but it didn't take a genius to imagine.

'Oh, I think I'll go to the office,' he said casually, reaching down to turn the doorknob.

She removed her hand from it quickly, to avoid any contact between them, then immediately hoped that he had not noticed her reaction.

'At this hour?'

'I have a lot of paperwork to clear before I can go anywhere. You aren't, believe it or not, the only one whose tidy little schedule has been interrupted.'

'I never said that I was,' she muttered.

'You don't have to. The implication was there in your voice. You always did have a way of saying much more with your silences than with your words.'

That piece of insight startled her. Had he noticed that? It was a trait which she herself was aware of. She thought of it as tact, because she knew that if she relentlessly said what was on her mind there would be quite a few people who would be unnecessarily offended by her remarks. So she often kept silent, allowing her thoughts to supply the missing bits in her conversations.

But no one had ever been aware of this ploy. He must, she now thought, be incredibly perceptive to have picked that up from their numerous but casual encounters over the years.

Perception along those lines made her uneasy. It made her think that he could read her mind, and she didn't like that sensation.

'Really?' she said blankly. 'I'll expect to hear from you a little later, then. If I'm not in, you can always leave a message on my answer machine.'

'Fine. But make sure you're around from this afternoon. I'll probably try and get us on the earliest flight after lunch.'

It wasn't a suggestion, it was a command. Be home after twelve or else.

She shut the door on him after he had gone and retired to her bedroom, where she spent the next hour trying to court sleep.

But it was difficult. She felt as though she had been abruptly swept up in a whirlwind and, now that she had been let down from it, she still couldn't quite manage to find her feet. One minute she was in control of things, her diary all planned out with her various jobs, her social life, if not buzzing, then ticking over. The next, everything had been turned upside-down and she was off on some foolish rescue mission with a man who, after all these years, could still succeed in making her feel acutely uncomfortable with herself.

And that made her cross. Why did he arouse that reaction in her? Was it because, in the enforced intimacy of her flat, the power of his personality had seeped into her and made her over-conscious of herself?

That had to be the explanation, she decided. In the past, she had seen Adam frequently enough, but always in the company of other people. When they had been alone, she had been usually waiting for Fiona to put in an appearance. She had been able to step back and view him with detachment, never putting herself in a situation where his presence could overwhelm her.

Tonight, though, it had been different. There had been no one else around to dilute the sheer force of his masculinity. She had been obliged to face him, one to one, and she had found her composure wanting.

All the more pathetic, she told herself with disgust, when he had made it clear that he found her quite unappealing as a member of the opposite sex. I don't care, she told herself philosophically, I'm no longer addicted to him. But she would have to watch herself. She had no intention of being tripped up by that stupid charm of his. That wouldn't do at all. She now had a plane trip and a car ride alone with him to contend with and, if she was going to sit through the whole thing in a state of nervous tension, then she would end up in need of medical treatment at the end of it all.

She finally drifted off to sleep and when she next opened her eyes it was after nine o'clock.

She had appointments. Two to cancel. She sprang out of bed, bustled into the lounge for her diary, and rang them both.

Mrs Rafferty, her first appointment, who wanted photographs of the interior of her house taken for inclusion in a book she was writing on stately homes, was easy enough to pacify. She had been working on her book for two years. A short delay in the photographs was not a matter of life or death.

Her second client, however, was somewhat harder to placate.

Mrs Molton was an irascible woman at the best of times. Now she listened while Christina made her excuses, then she bellowed down the line, 'This isn't good enough!'

'I'm sorry, Mrs Molton,' she said, 'but I'm afraid it's unavoidable.'

'Unavoidable? The word doesn't exist in my vocabulary!'

Christina could well believe that, thinking of her now. Thin, wiry, with a voice that could shatter glass.

'And what about the dogs? My little poopsies? Don't you think that it isn't stressful for them, having to pose for photographs? They're beautifully groomed. Today you would have got it right, I know it.'

Christina thought of her subjects, two corgis as irascible as their owner. Was it any wonder that this shoot was taking twice as long as it should have?

'I can rearrange you for next Tuesday,' she murmured, not wanting to stray on to the subject of the two infernal hounds.

'And I can always rearrange you, young lady!' Mrs Molton informed her testily down the line. 'You're not the only photographer in the world, you know. My niece may well have recommended you, but that doesn't mean that I have to employ you. The world,' she continued in a booming voice that belied her stature, 'is full of talented photographers. I'll allow myself and my poopsies to be rearranged just this once, but not again!'

Christina released a long sigh as she replaced the receiver.

Thank you, Adam Palmer, she thought. Now if I lose this job, however unchallenging it may be, I blame you entirely.

She spent a desultory morning throwing things into an overnight bag and lethargically reviewing some negatives for a job which she had undertaken a fortnight previously and which were due for submission to a magazine in a week's time, but her mind was working overtime.

She kept thinking of Adam. She thought of the way his body moved, the way his eyes were somehow fierce yet coolly mocking at the same time. Had she forgotten all that, she wondered, or had she shoved it to the back of her mind?

These were irritating questions. She was acting like the silly teenager she had been all those years ago. She was no longer a teenager and she liked to think of herself as too clever to let herself be swayed by a man's appearance. She might not be beautiful, but she was smart enough, and she wasn't about to abandon her good sense by letting him get under her skin.

She glared at the jumper in her hand and then threw it into the bag.

Weather report or no weather report, she was going to make sure that she travelled with an ample supply of thick clothing.

The man on the radio had self-confidently assured her that there would be no snow in Scotland, although conditions would be freezing, but weathermen had a talent for getting it wrong.

At three in the afternoon Adam called to inform her that they would be leaving in an hour and a half.

'Meet me at the airport,' he said in the quick tone of voice which implied that he had better things to do than converse with her over the phone. 'Take a taxi and charge it to my company.'

'Yes, my day's going just fine, thank you for asking,' Christina said sweetly. 'Usual sort of problems when one has to postpone commitments, but I won't bore you with the details. Thank you for asking, though. And yes, I can meet you at the airport for four-thirty. Any specific place, or shall I just aimlessly meander around in the hope that I spot you somewhere?'

She heard the impatient click of his tongue and grinned wickedly down the line. Poor Adam. Not much time for her now that he had got what he wanted. She wondered whether he was looking at his watch and wishing that this silly woman would get off the line. He always did have a restless streak in him that spared little time for what he considered frivolities.

Unless, of course, those frivolities concerned getting a woman into bed. Then he had all the time in the world to play his elaborate games of seduction. Or at least that was what she had gleaned from what she had seen of him in the company of women and from what Fiona had told her. Confidentially.

'I'm busy,' he told her bluntly. 'I don't have time to waste chatting. I'll meet you at the check-in counter.'

He promptly hung up with that and she glared at the telephone in her hand.

What manners. He was busy, was he? And what about her? She would have been busy if it weren't for him. Had he considered that? Fat chance.

She wondered how many of his lady friends were informed by him that he was busy and couldn't waste time chatting with them, and decided that she preferred his honesty after all. It was always nice knowing where you stood.

She dressed warmly for the trip up: jeans, boots, a jumper with another one in her holdall, and a duffel coat which zipped up the front. The entire outfit made her appear ten pounds heavier than she was and she grimaced at the reflection that stared back at her in the mirror.

There goes one of your few assets, she told the reflection—your figure. No one would guess that you had one under all of this.

But that really didn't bother her very much. She had become quite accustomed to her appearance and to the fact that she seldom if ever attracted second glances from members of the opposite sex.

Her boyfriends had all been men who had got to know her well before becoming interested in her physically, and frankly she would have preferred their friendship to remain on a platonic basis only most of the time. She disliked fighting off prospective suitors who did nothing to send her blood-pressure soaring.

No one will ever send your blood-pressure soaring, she informed the reflection. She thought about Greg, dashing Greg, who had come the closest to doing something to her blood-pressure. He was the image that she had resolutely shoved to the back of her mind for the past year. Not that she had been in love with him, but she could still taste the ashes in her mouth at his scathing comment when they broke up. Frigid, he had informed her, plain and frigid, a woman who should be grateful to be looked at twice. He had been turned on by her intellect and by the contacts she had had in her job, but, he had told her, stripped of those, she was nothing but a plain Jane without the wherewithal to hold a man's interest. If she had slept with him, or had introduced him to some useful people, or preferably both, then he might have consented to continue seeing her for a while longer, but in the absence of both these prerequisites she was, he had made it clear, not a very desirable option.

She tightened her lips and forced herself to push that unpleasant scene back into the shadows of her mind, where it belonged, as a silent warning to her.

You're destined to be a career woman, she told herself. Not that she saw anything wrong with that at all.

She loved what she did, and she considered herself lucky. What had been a teenage hobby had blossomed into a fulfilling profession when, at the age of seventeen, she had entered a photography competition and won a fully paid photography course and some impressive equipment, most of which she still relied on. She enjoyed her work and, if Mr Right didn't happen to bounce along on his white stallion, then it was hardly the end of the world.

Her mother would be disappointed, of course. She baked bread, made jam and had a desperately old-fashioned outlook on the role of women in society. But Christina could cope with that.

No, the closest she imagined she would get to ardour was watching Fiona's antics from the sidelines.

She thought of Adam and frowned. Why had his image popped into her head just like that, without warning?

Because, she told herself, it was time to go. She gathered her belongings together, tried one last time to tune in to some weather news and failed, and edgily sat down to await the arrival of the taxi, which arrived promptly.

And Adam, she was heartened to see, was also waiting for her at the check-in counter. He had his back to her, chatting to the woman behind the desk, and she stopped for a few seconds to look at him.

He really was aggressively male, she thought with detachment. All broad-shouldered and slim-hipped, which made him look as though he spent hours working out. If she remembered correctly, though, he exercised very little.

Fate had seen fit to endow him with a body that somehow managed to stay perfectly tuned even if he did nothing about it.

She took a deep breath and walked up to the counter, noticing that the woman to whom he had been chatting, an attractive brunette, impeccably made up and with a hairstyle that looked as though each strand of hair had been individually glued into place, was not quite as warm when her attention was directed towards her as she was when it had been directed towards Adam.

'I hope you haven't been waiting too long,' Christina said, turning to Adam with a polite smile.

'Ten minutes,' he replied, 'but don't worry about it. I haven't been bored.'

Christina glanced at the brunette, now busily attending to some paperwork, and thought, I'll bet you haven't been bored. 'I wasn't worried about it,' she said in a saccharin-sweet voice, 'and I'm sure you haven't been bored.'

There was a wicked little smile in his eyes at her tone, even though his face remained serious, and she ignored it.

'Have you checked us in?'

He nodded and took her by the elbow, an instinctive gesture that made her body tense until she told herself that she was being silly. Again.

The brunette had looked up and was now pouting regretfully at him. She hoped he had a wonderful flight and an enjoyable stay in Scotland. When next he was around, he must promise to come to her counter; she would take some time off and treat him to a cup of coffee.

What a pretty sight, Christina thought, looking at the other woman. Was she as amenable towards all her passengers?

Then she looked at Adam, who was treating the brunette to some of that limitless charm of his, and she tapped her foot impatiently.

'How subtle you are,' he drawled as they moved away into the crowds. 'I'm surprised you didn't add looking at your watch and yawning to your little foot-tapping routine.'

He guided her effortlessly through the terminal, hardly looking around him at all. It was easy to see that he was a seasoned traveller, but that didn't come as a surprise to her. He owned and virtually single-handedly ran a massive publishing network, and she knew that he travelled world-wide on business throughout the year.

They glanced up at the departures board and Christina saw with relief that they were due to board the shuttle. At least that would cut down on time spent at the airport terminal.

'You looked,' she said, following on from his sarcastic observation, 'as though you were about to spend the rest of the day chatting to the brunette.' If not the night, she added uncharitably to herself.

Adam threw her a sidelong glance, which she felt rather than saw, since she steadfastly kept her eyes averted.

'I was merely killing time, waiting for you, and being polite in the process.'

'Polite? Oh, so that's your definition of being polite. Chatting up women.'

'Don't you get high-handed with me,' he said in a hard voice. 'You may drink your cocoa and go to bed by nine, but please don't assume that the rest of the world follows suit and that if they don't they're somehow debauched.'

Christina reddened. How dared he tell her off as though she were a six-year-old child! She refrained from saying anything, though. She had to survive the next few hours in his company, undiluted, and there was no point in starting off with an argument.

'How are we going to get from the airport in Glasgow to the cottage?' she asked stiffly. He had released her arm and was walking in long strides so that she had to half run to keep pace with him.

'I've arranged a car,' he said tersely. 'My subsidiary in Glasgow has a stock of company cars. Someone will drop it off and we can drive straight from the airport.'

'Convenient,' she murmured. 'Are you going to be up to the drive? Did you actually go to the office after you left me?'

She was panting a little, which didn't sound terribly dignified, especially as he was barely exerting himself, and was relieved when they finally reached their gate and slowed down to allow for control checks before they boarded the plane.

There were quite a few people on the flight. Ninety-nine per cent of them were businessmen, clutching their *Financial Times* and looking harassed.

'Yes,' Adam said, 'in answer to both your questions.'

They passed through and made their way to the plane.
'So you haven't slept since . . .'

'A while back,' he finished drily. 'But you needn't
fear that I'm going to fall asleep at the wheel. I'm quite
accustomed to getting very little sleep and functioning
adequately on it.'

She could believe that. He didn't look in the least
harassed. If anything, the thick cream jumper, the dark
trousers and the jacket slung casually over his arm made
him look in the peak of health and fighting fit. He
looked, in fact, terrifically well rested. Christina knew
that if she had gone for a day and a half without sleep
she would resemble one of the living dead.

The flight was short. She sat next to the window,
staring outside, and next to her Adam dozed. No doubt
he would wake up as refreshed as if he had had eight
hours' sleep.

She wasn't looking forward to the drive to the cottage.
She remembered it from years back as being long and
uncomfortable, a network of tiny roads that threatened
to taper out into dead ends at any minute. She doubted
they would have improved vastly in the intervening years.
It was an isolated spot, and isolated spots were not normally earmarked for super road systems.

In fact the bumpy journey at the age of thirteen had
been quite a highlight. Now, with just Adam and her
own awkward feelings for company, she suspected that
that would not be the case.

The company representative was waiting for them as
soon as they emerged from the terminal. Christina eyed
him drily as he bowed and scraped in front of Adam,
showing them to a Range Rover which had been located
specifically just in case the weather turned.

'It won't,' Christina assured him. 'Adam has given
instructions that it's to stay dry.'

The young boy blushed, unsure as to what response this remark called for, and Adam gave her an amused little grin.

'Now you've sent the poor chap away confused as hell,' he murmured to her as they settled into the car and glided smoothly out of the compound.

'Have I?' she responded in an innocent voice, staring through the window at the dreary, wind-blasted scenery flashing past and wishing she was back in London photographing Mrs Molton's two temperamental corgis. 'And I thought you really had had a word with higher powers and given instructions for the weather pattern over the next three days. You disappoint me, Adam.'

'Do I? You don't disappoint me. You still have the ability to make me laugh even when I'm cold and tired and on a trip which I'd rather not be doing.'

Christina looked at him, surprised. Did he really find her humorous? He had never given any indication of that before.

She didn't know whether to be flattered or vaguely insulted. Do I really want to be seen as some kind of stand-up comic, she wondered, or would I rather be viewed as someone attractive and sexy?

She frowned, confused that she should even be thinking about Adam Palmer considering her sexy. Sexy, of all things. There was about as much chance of that as of Mrs Molton giving her corgis up for adoption.

Besides, she didn't care one way or another what he thought of her. Once upon a time she had, but she had since learnt that fairy-tales and reality were poles apart, and that a girl with her lack of looks was destined to forge a career and leave the posing to other, more beautiful models.

'Let's hope it's worth it,' she replied impassively, ignoring his personal remark and concentrating on getting the conversation on to a safer topic. 'Fiona can be stubborn and she isn't going to like being followed around by her big brother.'

'Which is why you're here. She values your opinion.'

'Oh, great,' Christina muttered with a sigh, 'as if I'm any authority on relationships.'

'Aren't you?' He gave her a swift sidelong glance. 'I gathered from my sister that in between the cups of cocoa and the early nights your love-life wasn't exactly non-existent.'

'I beg your pardon?' she gagged, going bright red and swearing to throttle Fiona as soon as she could lay her hands on her. 'No, don't repeat your remark. I heard it perfectly well, and I can only say that it's none of your business.'

'True,' he agreed. 'Call it natural curiosity.'

'There's nothing natural about wanting to pry into my private life just for the sake of small talk. And it's not curiosity, it's nosiness. I don't ask you about what you do with those women of yours.'

'No, you make lots of generalisations instead.'

This was getting out of hand. She reached down and fiddled with the dials on the radio until she tuned in to one of the local channels.

'Is that a hint?'

'No,' she said with heavy sarcasm, 'I'm genuinely interested in the farming news.'

She pursed her lips and looked out of the window, and next to her she could feel him grinning like a damned Cheshire cat and she wanted to hit him. Hard.

Two more hours, she thought with a groan, two more hours before we get there.

CHAPTER THREE

AT LEAST the weather was fine. It was freezing cold, though beautifully warm inside the car, and with that crisp clarity that marked a fine British winter's day.

The farming news eventually gave way to a programme on classical music, which Christina rather enjoyed, and she focused her attention on the scenery outside. The trees were bare of leaves and as they left civilisation behind the landscape took on a bleak, rugged beauty that was awe-inspiring rather than appealing.

The main roads petered out into a series of much smaller roads, which the Range Rover handled well, although, with darkness rapidly descending, Adam was concentrating hard on the driving, the lines on his face grim as he manoeuvred the car round bends and down the twisty lanes.

What a place to pick, Christina thought. Hardly Fiona's style, and not at all up Simon's alley, if she had read him correctly. He was more the sort who liked hanging around the smart set, and a cottage in the middle of nowhere could hardly qualify as that.

The thoughts drifted through her head as they drove in silence, but not an uncomfortable one.

It was quite dark by the time they finally made it to their destination.

The cottage was set down a narrow path and overlooked a loch. It was beautiful in spring and summer, but eerie in the depths of winter.

As the car slowed down to accommodate the erratic nature of the path, Christina leaned forward in her seat and peered around her, trying to see beyond the patches of landscape illuminated by the headlamps of the car.

Outside, she could almost hear the silence. It was a nerve-racking feeling, especially after London. A bit, she imagined, like being whipped into the black hole, lost in time and space.

She laughed nervously and turned to Adam.

'Spooky, don't you think? I can remember thinking that last time I was here with Fiona and your parents, and it hasn't changed.'

'It has got a timeless quality about it,' he concurred absent-mindedly, driving dead slow now. 'Don't you find that charming?'

'I find that off-balancing,' Christina said honestly. 'I think I've become far too accustomed to all the noise and chaos in London.'

'A city girl,' he murmured, making it sound like an insult.

'It's where the work is,' she responded tartly, wishing she hadn't bothered to try and make conversation.

They lapsed into silence and she waited to see the impact of the cottage as they cleared the final bend. Its location had always impressed her. It was so startling against the deserted landscape, like a beacon keeping watch over the loch, guarding against evil spirits.

They turned the bend and the very first thing she noticed was that the cottage was in pitch-darkness. She felt her stomach plummet and a sick feeling of dreadful anticipation rose up into her throat. Adam was frowning heavily. He stopped the car outside the front door and looked at her.

'I don't see any lights, do you?'

Christina didn't answer. She was desperately trying to make out if there was a car parked at the side of the house, but she couldn't see a thing. No car, no lights. No Fiona.

'Perhaps they've popped out for a minute,' she said feebly.

'Popped out? Where? Down to the local nightclub? There's nowhere around here to pop out to, is there?'

He stared at her impatiently, his eyes glittering in the darkness inside the car, and she felt her temper flare.

'Shall we go in?' she asked, trying to keep a polite face on things. She pulled down the door-handle and opened the door, not giving him the chance to hurl any more accusations at her.

Besides—who knew?—Fiona and Simon might well be inside the cottage. With the lights out. Having a romantic evening. Maybe their car was parked at the back. Maybe, maybe, maybe. She knew that she was clutching at straws, because a little part of her desperately did not want to be here, alone, with a man who could still make her pulse race however hard she told herself not to be a fool.

She heard him slam his own car door behind him and she didn't look around. She stood by the front door, patiently waiting for him to unlock it, which he did with a grim expression on his face.

He pushed open the door, to an isolated and freezing cold cottage, and then turned to her.

'Well, so much for your bloody girlish confidences. No sign of life here, or did you deliberately bring me here on a wild-goose chase?' He didn't give her the time to answer. He switched on the lights, and then began walking briskly out of the door.

Christina raced behind him and yelled out, 'Where are you going?'

No reply. He heaved their cases out of the back seat and then strode back inside.

'Don't worry, much as I'm tempted to leave you here after having led me here on this wasted trip, rest assured that I won't.'

He dumped the cases on the ground and she followed him into the tiny kitchen, furious that he was blaming her for this. Her! As if she had dragged him kicking and screaming out here! As if she had held a gun to his head and demanded his co-operation! When in fact it had been the other way around!

'I did not lead you here! And I resent your implication that this——' she gesticulated to the deserted cottage '—that this is all my fault!'

'Well, whose fault is it? You told me that this was where she was, didn't you? Or maybe that was just a little ploy to get me up here when you knew perfectly well that Fiona was somewhere else, probably a thousand miles away in the opposite direction! I was crazy to have believed a word you said. I might have guessed that you were in cahoots with my sister. Who knows? Maybe it was your idea that they take off. Maybe all that sincere concern about Fiona and Simon and their incompatibility was just a clever front. After all, clever is the one thing you are. And still waters run deep, so they say!' He looked at her narrowly until she began to feel giddy. What was he thinking?

'Or maybe,' he continued, his voice as hard as ice and cold with speculation, 'there was another reason you dragged me up here.'

He let that provocative remark hang in the air until she snapped nervously, 'What on earth are you talking about?'

'Can't you guess?' His lips curled cynically. 'Maybe you got me up here because you thought that in this isolated splendour you might be able to pick up the strands of the relationship which you wanted all those years ago, and which never got off the ground.'

She could feel the colour drain out of her face, and somewhere at the back of her mind she knew that she was trembling, on the brink of losing control. But that she wouldn't do. Let him insinuate whatever he liked.

'I won't bother to answer that. I'll only say that you have the biggest ego I've ever seen if you could think that——'

'You still want me after all these years?'

'Yes! I . . .' She took a deep, steadying breath. 'How was I to know that Fiona decided against coming here?'

'Female intuition? Or is that one of those things missing in your life?'

There was a deadly silence and then Christina flushed. One of those things missing in your life. One of how many things? Looks, perhaps. Sex appeal. Was that what he was referring to? Were those the other things missing from her life?

He pulled down two mugs from the cupboard and she watched in silence as he poured them both some coffee, then proceeded to sit at the kitchen table drinking it, cradling the mug in his hands.

Neither of them had removed their coats and after a while he said neutrally, 'I'll have to get some logs in and do something about lighting a fire or else we'll both freeze to death here.'

Christina wished that she could summon up the self-control to respond to him, but his implied insult, his fantastic speculations, had winded her. Instead she continued to watch him covertly over the rim of her mug, taking in his strong hands, the width of his shoulders, the powerful body.

He inspired confidence. However dynamic and impressive he was in the field of business, that did not mean that he could not cope in a situation such as this. If he said that he would get logs and make this place warm, then he would do so, even if it meant felling a tree in the process. Somehow, from somewhere, he would find the ability to perform the impossible.

That was one of the things that had drawn her to him from as far back as she could remember: that unspoken talent of his that made you feel as though he were capable of anything. Even when she had grown up and cool logic had replaced her girlhood crush, telling her that no one was capable of everything, she still believed, deep down, that he could achieve what few men could.

Was that what all those other women saw in him? That strength?

How pitiful, she suddenly thought, joining ranks with his brainless bimbo followers as if it were the most natural thing in the world. God, he would have a field-day if he could read her mind; he would die laughing. He would think that his crazy remarks about her having enticed him up here under false pretences so that she could make a pass at him were spot-on.

She forced herself to speak and gathered her wayward thoughts into order. 'We could always turn around and go home.'

'Don't be ridiculous. We'd never make it to the airport in time to catch a flight back to Heathrow, and anyway, there's no way that I'm getting into that car and driving for another two hours without having rested first.'

Christina sighed and sat down opposite him. The cold was beginning to bite its way through her coat. She wished that she had worn her gloves instead of leaving them behind in the flat.

'I'm sorry that you undertook this trip for nothing,' she said quietly, 'but I didn't make you come, despite what you choose to think.'

'No, you didn't.' He raked his fingers through his hair and sat back, his head thrown back, his eyes closed. He looked tired, for the first time since they had set off.

'Shall I fix us something to eat?'

He looked at her. 'There won't be much choice. Old Frank, who keeps an eye on this place from time to time, makes sure that there's some food in the cupboards, but it's all basic stuff.'

She stood up with a stiff smile, relieved that some normality had been re-established between them. Small, inconsequential talk was just what she needed. 'That's all right, believe me. Quite often I don't eat at all, if I'm particularly busy.'

She had her back to him and was rummaging through the cupboard, extracting anything promising.

'I can see that,' he murmured. 'You're very thin.' She felt his words race up her spine like a warm touch, making her stiffen for just a fraction of a second.

She wasn't going to let him get under her skin, though, so she pretended that his remark was not worthy of an answer. Instead she asked him where he was going to get the logs.

'The shed outside.' He stood up and stretched, a long, lazy movement that a cat would make. 'Let's hope they're not too damp to light.' He came close to her, so that his voice was by her ear. 'Or else we might have to think of alternative ways of keeping warm.'

Christina turned on him sharply. 'Over my dead body,' she bit out, and he laughed.

'Little joke. No need to rise up in arms. As I said, your maidenly honour is perfectly safe with me.' He left the kitchen, still chuckling under his breath, and she thought, Very funny, very hysterical. He might find his brand of humour highly amusing, but it left her cold.

His comment had been patronising. She wasn't a sex kitten by any stretch of the imagination, certainly nothing that would catch his fancy, and she resented his sly innuendo, which was really just an attempt to laugh at her. Like his remarks about her drinking cocoa. Little gibes at her expense. She hoped he developed a severe case of frost-bite out there. Oh, she would see the funny side of that all right.

She slammed around a few tins, making an effort to be creative with their limited supply and then abandoning the attempt. Baked beans, corned beef and tinned macaroni cheese would never constitute a gourmet meal, however artistically she arranged the ingredients.

She heard the front door slam shut and busied herself all the more in the kitchen while, out of the corner of her eye, she watched him remove his waterproof jacket and set to work on making a fire. His movements were quick and assured. Had he done a course on this sort of thing? In under fifteen minutes there was a fire burning, taking the edge off the biting chill in the cottage.

Christina removed her coat, and then her jumper. When he strode into the kitchen a few minutes later the food was on the table.

'It was the best I could do,' she said defensively, before he could make the expected remark. They both stared at the concoction on the plates and she felt the corners of her mouth twitch.

'Basic fare,' he said, sitting down. 'Beans are very good for us. Lots of fibre.'

She sat opposite him and grinned reluctantly. 'If I were a cordon bleu cook I could have turned this into something a bit more appetising.'

'And spoil the challenge of finding out whether it tastes as basic as it looks?' He grinned back at her and it struck her again how potent a male animal he was. There was arrogance and aggression in the hard lines of his face, but when he smiled those hard lines could seem staggeringly charming. 'Actually,' he said conversationally, 'it makes a change to find a woman who isn't dying to get into my kitchen and start proving to me what a wonderful cook she is.'

Christina raised one eyebrow. 'Aren't you the lucky one?' she mocked. 'I don't know of too many men who would turn that away.'

He shrugged. 'Depends whether you want a woman getting under your feet, doesn't it?'

Good grief, she thought, what a heart of gold this man had. Good thing he had the funds to wine and dine his women and not have to endure them cluttering up his kitchen.

'Have you ever got under a man's feet?' he asked in the same casual voice, his eyes on his food.

'I hope not,' she answered in an equally casual voice, even though she found this digression into her personal life very disquieting. 'I would hate to think that I was anyone's doormat. That fire's really coming along, isn't it?'

'Nothing like a real fire. And you've never fallen head over heels in love with anyone? Not even . . . what's his name . . . Jim? Gary? Oh, no, now I remember—Greg. I understand from a mutual acquaintance that he actually disturbed the smooth ripples of your life.'

'Fiona had no right to discuss my private life with you,' she bit out, mortified.

'Maybe she didn't consider it a secret. Was it?'

'Was it what?' Her heart was beating painfully, and looking at him with any semblance of calm was costing her a great deal of effort. She wasn't one to talk about herself, and least of all to this particular man.

'A secret. Were you ashamed of him?'

'Of course not!' she lied vehemently. 'Why should I be?'

'Well, I would hardly call Greg Robinson the sort of man that every mother longs for for her daughter.'

Christina was beginning to feel dizzy. She wanted to close her eyes and pretend that this conversation wasn't taking place, but she couldn't, not when his eyes were boring through her.

'You know him?' she asked faintly, and he nodded, not taking his eyes off her face.

'He tried to involve Fiona in a relationship a while back—quite a while back. When that failed he began dropping hints to her about wanting to climb into my social scene, and that was when I started taking a personal interest in him. I discovered that he's quite unscrupulous. I guess that was why Fiona told me when you started going out with him. She was worried for you, but she didn't feel that she could say anything to you. After all, what is it they say? That the bearer of bad tidings always takes the blame?'

Christina's mouth was too dry to find an answer to that. Not only did Adam Palmer know all about her private life, but he knew more about it, in a way, than she did. Another wave of sickening humiliation washed over her and she hated him for that.

'I don't see what these revelations have got to do with anything,' she said in a strangled voice.

'I merely wondered whether that had anything to do with the way you're so absorbed in your work.'

'I'm absorbed in my work because I happen to enjoy it,' she countered, forcing herself to look at him politely, blankly. 'Greg was a mistake, I can't deny that, but we all make them. One thing I can say is that he taught me a lesson. I'm immune to so-called male charm and good looks.' She gave him a cool, pointed smile even though her mouth felt stiff with the effort of it. She closed her knife and fork and carried her plate to the sink, carefully washing it and stacking it on the draining board.

'What time do you think we can leave tomorrow?' She dried her hands and stood looking at him, her arms folded.

'You don't like me asking questions of a personal nature, do you?' he said, tilting his chair back and clasping his hands behind his head.

Those bright blue eyes caught hers and held them until she felt her legs go shaky.

'Does anyone?' she threw the question back at him.

'We've known each other for years,' he said, and she wondered whether he expected her to concur that their long-standing familiarity gave him the right to question her.

'I don't follow you.'

'Don't you? Then you're not as clever as I thought.'

She wished he would stop staring at her. It made her feel horribly self-conscious, too aware of her physical shortcomings for her own liking.

She was sure that he was measuring her against the women he knew and finding her wanting, and the thought made her cringe.

Of course I don't care, she told herself severely. I stopped caring what Adam Palmer thought of me a long time ago. It was his attitude, she convinced herself, that she didn't care for. He had been patronising her when he had mentioned Greg, laughing at her, she was sure of it. There wasn't much to do here, isolated in this cottage, and the devil would always find work for idle hands.

Was it any surprise that he made her feel flustered and hot under the collar?

She reached out for his plate, asking him whether he was finished, and he caught her by the wrist. The movement was so sudden that she froze for an instant, then she wriggled to snatch her hand away.

'I'm not going to bite you,' he murmured, amused.

'Let me go!'

He was as strong as she had thought. Her efforts to pull herself free were as good as useless.

He released her and she flew back, her brown hair swinging against her face. Her cheeks were bright red and she wanted to cry with anger and embarrassment, but she wasn't going to give him the satisfaction of knowing how much that brief physical contact had disturbed her.

She stood there, massaging her hand and willing her features to assume their normal cool expression.

'Why did you do that?' she asked evenly, and he gave her a lazy smile.

'I didn't want you washing my plate. I'm really not as much of a male chauvinist as you'd like to believe.' He stood up and walked across to the sink, whistling under his breath. 'You can go into the living-room. I'll bring you in some coffee.'

Christina hovered for a few seconds longer, then went into the living-room, to sit in one of the ancient but comfortable chairs by the fire.

The cottage was basically well built and comfortable. Over the years not much had been done to it. Bits and pieces had been replaced, but a lot of the furniture was the original pieces brought in when the place had first been bought.

She looked around her and wondered how often it had been used since Fiona's and Adam's parents had died. When they had been alive it had been used during the school vacations regularly, but that was—she wrinkled her nose and thought about it—at least seven years ago.

Fiona, she knew, rarely came up, and she was certain that Adam came no more frequently himself. He didn't strike her as the sort who found a cottage holiday in the wilds very tempting, and she couldn't imagine any of those women she had seen him with in the past putting up with this level of rusticity.

She was so engrossed in her thoughts that she wasn't aware of him until he handed her a mug of coffee; then he sat down opposite her, his long legs stretched out and crossed at the ankles.

'So what are you going to do about Fiona now?' she asked curiously, blowing on to the hot surface of the coffee and then taking tiny exploratory sips.

'What can I do? I have no idea where she is. I'll just have to wait until she decides to make an appearance, and in the meantime hope that that shifty bastard doesn't talk her into marriage.'

'She has got a choice in the matter,' Christina pointed out, relaxing a bit now that they were on neutral ground, and he looked at her blankly. Not if I had my way, was what he was probably thinking, she decided wryly.

'When have you ever known my sister to be rational about anything?'

Christina thought about that one. 'She did take that secretarial course,' she suggested finally.

'On my insistence. I felt it was important for her to achieve some measure of financial independence, even though there was no necessity for it. People need to focus their lives on something if they're to have any purpose.'

'I agree with you.' For once, she thought.

'I realise that,' he drawled. 'I'd say your life has never lacked purpose at any point. You worked hard at school, worked hard at college, and now you're working hard at your photography.'

'You make that sound like an insult,' Christina said stiffly, her hackles rising again.

'I admire it.'

Admirable, she thought, but unattractive. Wasn't it funny how easily men could categorise women? There was the wife, the mistress and then the career woman. And the career woman was invariably the one who lost out on the sex appeal.

'Thank you,' she said blandly. 'I like to think that I put everything into my work. It's a competitive field. I could never afford to sit back and keep my fingers crossed that jobs were going to come in.'

'So how exactly do you get your work?' he asked, placing his empty mug on the table next to him and folding his hands on his lap.

'Word of mouth most of the time.'

This was the first time they had ever really spoken about what she did. Normally they held fleeting, polite conversations in the company of other people. Talking to him now, with his attention unwaveringly focused on her and no one else, made her feel oddly uneasy—as if she was giving a little bit of herself away, as if that in itself was something which she knew she ought not to do.

'We might be able to make use of you on some of our shoots,' he said, and she could feel herself suddenly become defensive.

'There's no need. I have plenty of work. I wasn't hinting.'

'I never said that you were,' he pointed out mildly, the blue eyes hooded as he looked at her. 'We normally use our own team of people, but who knows? One of our magazines isn't doing as well as it should. Perhaps a different perspective might do something to change that.'

Christina smiled politely and didn't say anything. Adam owned a massive publishing chain which incorporated a wide cross-section of magazines, all of them expensive and glossy. When she had first started out Fiona had suggested that she use him to get her foot on the ladder, but she had refused. That smelt a bit of asking for favours for the wrong reasons, and her pride would not allow her to do it.

So she had quietly built up her own clientele. It had been hard work, but over the years she had managed and she was proud of her achievement. She wasn't about to be enticed by Adam Palmer into doing shoots for one of his spin-offs because he perhaps felt sorry for her. Poor plain little Christina, struggling hard in her career, burying herself in her job after a disastrous, embarrassing relationship with a man who was obviously known to all and sundry as a cad—all and sundry, that was, except her. Why not throw her a kind hand-out? No, thank you.

So she sipped from her now lukewarm coffee and refrained from saying anything.

This wasn't the response that he had expected from her. His mouth narrowed into a faintly impatient line and he said aggressively, 'Well, wouldn't you like to do a spot of work for my company? I guarantee that the pay would be excellent.'

'I'm sure it would be,' she hedged.

'You'll have to let me see your portfolio.'

'Sure,' she murmured vaguely, averting her eyes from his. She pretended to stifle a yawn and stood up. 'Which bedroom do you want me to use?'

The cottage had three bedrooms, a legacy from when it was used by the entire family. They were quite small but comfortable.

'Whichever,' Adam said carelessly, and she had the feeling that he was still piqued by her dismissal of his offer. The thought brought a genuine smile to her lips. 'I've lit fires in two of them, so you can take your pick.'

'You're not going to sleep?'

'Presently,' he said in a dismissive voice, and she collected her holdall and then left him in the living-room, staring broodingly into the fire and thinking who knew what?

She used the bedroom which she remembered from years ago, the one she had shared with Fiona. It was exactly as she remembered it, and the very fact that it had not changed was delightful.

The wallpaper, a pattern of small lavender flowers, still adorned the walls and the bed was the same one, with the soft mattress dipping in the middle.

She washed her face at the sink in the bedroom, deciding that she would have a bath the following morning before they left, and then settled under the quilt cover, feeling wonderfully warm.

The cottage might lack central heating, but Adam had been right when he'd said that there was nothing like a real fire. The room glowed with it, and it was lovely to think of the cold outside, banished by the flames in the bedroom.

She pulled out her book which she had brought with her to read, but she didn't get far. After a while her eyelids began to feel heavy and she switched off the bedside lamp, lying in the darkness, sleepily aware that her thoughts were of Adam, which was irritating. Did he really think that she had contrived to get him up here so that she could have him to herself? A desperate woman who was on the rebound from a good-for-nothing charmer? Of course not, a logical voice inside her said. That's just his line in being provocative. It was a trait he had been born with. She had responded correctly, had refused to rise to the bait, but the insinuation still niggled away like a nasty insect under her skin.

She decided to think of Fiona instead. Where had she gone? Had she made the ultimate mistake of getting married to Simon behind her brother's back? If she had, then she obviously possessed enormous courage, because Christina personally couldn't think of anything more daunting than Adam in a rage. Not just angry, but in a real, unabatable rage.

There I go, she thought drowsily, thinking of that stupid man again.

Gradually she drifted into sleep. She had no idea what the time was when she next opened her eyes, but she knew that it wasn't morning. It was too black outside. Also the fire had not quite died.

Of course, it was the strangeness of the bed. She was too accustomed to sleeping in her own bed. The dip in the mattress, which had been a source of fun in her early teens, had given her a backache, and she slipped out from under the covers, shivering at the drop in temperature. She slipped on her robe and wandered out into the tiny corridor that led to the living-room and kitchen.

There was no milk in the cottage and the thought of coffee wasn't appealing. She would have to make do with a glass of water.

She tiptoed into the kitchen, fumbling to find a glass and quietly turning on the tap. She didn't want to make a sound and run the risk of waking Adam.

She was walking back to the bedroom when out of the corner of her eye she saw a figure lying on the chair, and she stopped in surprise.

It was Adam, asleep in the chair, his arms flung out on either side of him.

She edged across to where he was, fascinated at how youthful his face looked in repose. He was breathing quietly, not snoring at all, and there was something terribly appealing about him as he semi lay there on the chair.

She reached out and gave him a soft shake. He might look peaceful enough now, but once the fire had died completely he would catch his death of cold. She shook him again and bent towards him, so that her face was only inches away from his.

'Adam,' she whispered huskily. 'Adam, wake up. You have to go to your bed to sleep. You can't sleep here.'

He half opened his eyes and looked at her drowsily. In the darkness, she couldn't read the expression behind them, but she knew that he was disorientated at being awakened. She could feel it.

He must be as tired as hell, she thought with a twinge of sympathy, to have fallen asleep out here.

She wanted to reach out and stroke his face, and perhaps, she later thought, he read something of what was going through her mind, because he reached out and pulled her towards him, sighing as his lips found hers.

His kiss was warm and drowsy to start with, but then subtly it changed, becoming harder, his hands clasping in her hair, controlling her. His mouth became a hard, powerful force, parting her lips, drawing an urgent, heated response from her. She had never felt like this before. It was as if a wild beast lying inside her had been unlocked. Greg had kissed her—limp, long kisses that had bored her even though she had found him physically attractive.

She moaned, a tiny sound escaping against his mouth, and that seemed to fire the urgency of his kiss even further. His tongue forged a way into her mouth, then along her neck as he tilted her head back, half rising to prop himself up on one elbow.

Her breasts were aching, only inches away from his face, and she imagined what it would be like to feel his exploring tongue on them. It was an intimacy she had never known before, but the madness she was feeling made her want it with something close to desperation.

She never expected it, though, and when his mouth wetly and hungrily circled her nipple through her night-dress she jerked back in shock and confusion.

'What do you think you're playing at?' she asked, trembling. She faltered across the room and flicked the switch and light flooded the room. 'Are you mad?' she continued in a high voice. 'Kissing me like that... Making love...'

Her body was still throbbing where he had touched her, and in places where he hadn't, and she looked away from his face, only briefly registering his expression of surprise, whether at her rejection of him or his response to her she didn't question.

Then a shutter dropped over his face, and when she raised her eyes to his he was grim.

'For God's sake,' he bit out coldly, 'stop making a mountain out of a molehill. It was only a kiss. Not rape.'

'That's not the point! I don't expect to be mauled about by you!'

'Stop acting like a horrified virgin. You're no longer a teenager, you're a woman.'

That only stoked her anger yet further and when she opened her mouth sheer rage robbed her of a suitable retort.

'That doesn't give you the right to... to...'

He didn't answer but she could tell from the dark flush on his face that he caught her meaning well enough.

'You're over-reacting,' he muttered, standing up, and she shrank back automatically, realising that her unconscious gesture only made him grimmer.

You're a career woman, she desperately told herself; you're in control of your life. But here, in this darkened, remote room, she felt as though she was at the mercy of every unwelcome emotion, every wayward thought.

'No, I'm not!' she threw out wildly. 'You're all the same, you men!'

'Don't confuse me with that bum who seduced you into bed with him,' he responded tightly, moving towards her so that she fell back one more step, her back now pressed against the wall. Her anger, she realised, was now matched with his, except, where she was breathing thickly and in the grip of a dreadful sense of panic, he was cold and controlled.

'Why not?' she asked recklessly. 'You're a womaniser just like him, aren't you?'

'I don't exploit women!'

'No? Remind me to ask one of your many cast-offs to confirm that!'

They glared at each other in furious silence, then he said, in a curiously gentle voice, 'He must really have hurt you. Did he?'

His tone of voice brought a sudden lump to her throat and she stared at him with a helpless longing to pour everything out, despite the fact that she had positively loathed him only a few minutes before.

'He used me,' she said, looking away, 'and who likes being used?'

'No one,' he replied and she gave him a quick, searching look.

'Not that you speak from experience,' she offered shakily.

'You would be surprised,' he countered and before she could dwell on that he was turning away and reality was reasserting itself.

His back was still to her as she made her way up to her bedroom.

Tomorrow, she thought reasonably, settling under the thick blankets, things will be back to normal and this frightening, nightmarish feeling will subside. In fact, I'll probably laugh at myself.

She closed her eyes and waited for morning to rescue her.

CHAPTER FOUR

THE weather had turned an ominous grey the following morning, and it was with a sense of relief that Adam suggested they leave without delay. He was echoing her thoughts exactly.

'I can't afford to be trapped here if there's snow,' he said, looking out of the window with a frown. 'I have some very important meetings to go to tomorrow.'

I can think of a few other very good reasons why we shouldn't end up trapped here, Christina wanted to inform him, and most of them revolve around us getting on each other's nerves.

She still hadn't quite managed to forget the effect that kiss of his had had on her the previous night, the feel of his hands on her body, the ridiculously frightening sensation that that was what she had spent her life waiting for, but she wasn't going to let it continue to absorb her thoughts. Nor was she going to analyse what her reactions to it indicated. The minute she started along that road, anyway, her mind sheered away from it like a terrified horse rearing up in self-defence.

And that suited her just fine, because there was no point in introspection of that nature, was there? Thinking about it wouldn't help her to reach any conclusions. After her traumatic relationship with Greg, she had wasted far too many hours, nights, dwelling on their break-up, coming back time and time again to his final, parting insults, and what had that achieved? It had filled her with the sour taste of bitterness. The only good thing to have emerged from it was her resolution to steer well clear of involvement in the foreseeable future. Of course the mere idea of involvement with Adam Palmer was laughable anyway. He was as ill suited to her as she was to him, a fact which he had made patently clear the evening before.

The fact that they had stupidly done something which she would have been the first to admit had been a massive error of judgement had been just one of those things, a product of unusual circumstance, to be put to the back of one's mind and eventually laid to rest.

They drove most of the journey to the airport in silence. Christina anxiously watched the skies as the car weaved along the small roads, only breathing a sigh of relief when they were on the motorway.

'I suppose,' Adam said, as they later boarded the plane, 'you're quite glad that this proved to be a futile journey. You disapproved of it from the start.'

Christina shrugged. 'I don't suppose, thinking about it, that we would, either of us, have achieved anything if Fiona and Simon had been there. You can't tell other people how to run their lives, even if you're convinced that they would benefit from it.'

She closed her eyes and tried to ignore the fact that he was staring at her.

She looked a mess, she knew that. They had decided to leave before she could have the luxury of a shower, and she was feeling unkempt. Her hair, which she had clipped back, had escaped in strands, limp, mousy strands which she irritably kept pushing back from her face.

'You could be right,' Adam agreed, and her eyes flew open in surprise.

'I could?' She looked at him drily. 'You mean we agree on something? What is the world coming to?'

He frowned. 'We could probably agree on a lot more if you weren't so damned defensive and prickly all the time.'

'Funny that I'm only that way when I'm in your company, wouldn't you say?' She gave him a sweet smile which did nothing to re-establish his sense of humour.

'Hysterical. I must be losing my touch with the opposite sex.'

His expression was perfectly serious, but she had a feeling that somewhere he was laughing at her, and she found that unsettling. Was that some snide way of reminding her that, despite what she said, his touch with the opposite sex had been all too successful with her the night before?

'That's the most egotistical thing I've ever heard,' she said, choosing to take his words at face value. 'And it's damned chauvinistic as well! Are you implying that all you need to do is turn on the charm and women drop like ninepins?'

He laughed aloud. 'It's so easy to get you standing on that soapbox of yours, preaching to me about my demon ways.'

Christina looked at him and ground her teeth together.

He was right, though, he seemed capable of playing her like a musical instrument, riling her and then watching with amusement to see her reactions. She, however, didn't find it amusing at all.

She maintained a stony silence until the plane landed at Heathrow, and in the ensuing chaos of disembarking and clearing Customs she didn't have the time for polite small talk.

Once outside the airport terminal, he turned to her, though, and asked whether he could give her a lift back to her flat.

'I left my car in the long-stay car park.'

Christina shook her head. 'No, thanks. I'm fine with a taxi back. I wouldn't,' she found herself adding, 'want to take up any of your precious time.'

He gave her an impatient look and she could have kicked herself.

'Fine.' He looked at his watch with a little frown. 'Well, in that case, I'll leave you here. Thanks for coming up to Scotland with me, even if it was an abortive mission. It did have the advantage of throwing us together, though. Made me realise what a long time it's been since we had any kind of conversation together.' He gave her a lazy smile that made her heart lurch oddly. 'Or any kind of... anything... come to that.'

She blushed, wondering whether she should apologise for that. He certainly made it sound as though their disagreements had all been her making, which was ludicrous.

She held out her hand awkwardly and he took it briefly, before withdrawing his hand to glance at his watch.

'We must get together some time,' he murmured, but already his attention was wandering. He was no doubt planning the day's activities, thinking of his very important meetings, his very important life. She nodded politely and followed him with her eyes for a few seconds as he strode off in the opposite direction.

His sudden disappearance left her with a curiously empty feeling, and she shook her head impatiently, turning around and looking for a taxi.

It seemed funny going back to her flat. She felt as though an awful lot had taken place over the last twenty-four hours or so, yet when she thought about it nothing really had happened. She had gone on a wild-goose chase with a man who had rubbed her up the wrong way, and that was about the size of it. That little episode in the middle of the night counted for nothing, was laughable really, and the fact that he had told her a few home truths about her ex-boyfriend had embarrassed her at the time, but in fact it had been quite good in restoring her lack of faith in the opposite sex.

There were two messages waiting for her on her answering machine when she got back. One was from a prospective employer, and she made a quick note of what he wanted, so that she could brush up on the relevant information before she called him back.

The other call was from Fiona. At home and dying for a chat.

Christina called the house immediately and the telephone was answered after two rings.

'Where have you been?' she opened without preamble. 'Your brother and I have been haring up and down the country looking for you, so that he could straighten you out.'

Fiona sounded in a jubilant mood. She giggled and said breathlessly, 'Honestly, Chrissie, it's a good job I changed my mind about going up there, isn't it? Can't you keep a secret? I told you not to tell Adam. You know what he's like!'

'I had no intention of telling him anything,' Christina objected, 'but he steamrollered me into it with a mixture of persuasion and blackmail.'

'I can understand that.' Fiona's voice was rueful. 'I've had it all my life. Well, ever since Mum and Dad died, anyway.'

'So?' Christina prompted, settling herself comfortably on the floor, cross-legged. 'What the hell is happening between you and Simon?'

There was a pause, then Fiona said in as serious a voice as Christina had heard from her in a long time, 'It's all off. We flew over to Paris. I paid, of course.

And, well, we had a long talk, over a very expensive dinner, which I paid for as well. I think I must have had misgivings before then, but things he said…' She sighed. 'He was obviously banking on me, counting on my money. He even began talking about investments, and how much he would plough into his career!'

'Poor Fiona,' Christina said sympathetically.

'Lucky Fiona. Adam was right. He always is. Isn't it depressing? I've really learnt a lesson from this experience, believe me. Never again.'

'No more men?'

Fiona laughed. 'Well, never say never. But tell me, how did you and Adam get along? Must have been a nasty shock arriving at that cottage in the middle of nowhere to find yourselves alone. Or was it? You can tell Aunty Fi.'

All of a sudden, it seemed time to conclude the conversation. She muttered something vague about it being an experience, and hoped that her friend would desist from too many questions. Fiona could be remarkably perceptive at times, and there was a stubborn streak in her, as in her brother, which could be very tenacious when roused.

But she had too much on her mind to pursue the topic. They rang off with a promise to see each other the following week, and Christina promptly submerged herself in her work. Mrs Molton, the wretched dogs, this new job, negatives which needed looking at for deadlines which were fast approaching.

That was the stuff of her life. A couple of nights a week she met up with various of her girlfriends. They had a meal together, or went to a wine bar for a drink. It was relaxing, and ever since Greg Robinson it had been all she had needed.

She had her work: she was still building up her clientele. Adam had been spot-on in saying that she had submerged herself in her job, but it didn't bother her in the slightest. Why should it? Her work would always be the one constant in her life. The Gregs—not that there would ever be another mistake like that—of this world could come and go.

She caught herself thinking of Adam. How was it, she wondered, that he had never settled down? It wasn't through lack of choice, and surely there came a time in one's life when playing the field became an empty pastime and you needed the stability of a normal, committed relationship? She couldn't ever remember him being involved with a woman to that degree, and if he had been Fiona would have been sure to tell her about it. She forced herself out of her speculations, annoyed that she had been all but daydreaming about him, which just went to prove how much he got under her skin.

She was in a particularly good mood the following week when she met Fiona. She had managed to eradicate Adam Palmer almost completely from her consciousness, Mrs Molton's two dogs had consented to being photographed, and the potential job had turned into a lucrative reality.

Fiona was waiting for her. There was a glow about her that Christina recognised and she wondered whether her friend was in love. Again.

But no. They had a drink, deliberated over the choices on the Mexican menu, and Fiona assured her that there were no men on the scene at all.

'I'm still recovering from Adam's last attack of brotherly possessiveness over Simon,' she admitted, and Christina said casually,

'And how is he?'

Fiona gave her a shrewd look, which Christina successfully dodged by concentrating on her food. 'Fine. Our paths haven't crossed much recently.' She giggled. 'Probably still recuperating from my "disgusting behaviour", as he called it.'

'He does have a way with words,' Christina murmured. 'Never one to beat about the bush.'

'No. He tells me you argued the whole time you were together. Did you?'

'I believe there were a few peaceful interludes,' Christina hedged. What else had he said about her? she wondered. Nothing flattering, she could well imagine.

'What did you argue about?'

Christina shrugged her shoulders. 'This and that,' she said vaguely, changing the subject, because that image of him which she had managed to eradicate was threatening to resurface in a most irritating manner.

They kept the conversation general after that, but Fiona clearly still had it on her mind, because as they turned to go their separate ways she said suddenly, 'You're invited to a party. It's Adam's birthday a week on Saturday and I'm having a bit of a surprise bash for him.'

'You've never done anything like that before,' Christina said, surprised and a little taken aback.

'No,' Fiona agreed readily. 'But his next birthday is a big one.'

'And...?'

'And,' Fiona continued gleefully, 'he'll absolutely hate it. I mean, he'll hate walking into the house and being greeted by hundreds of people.'

'Getting your own back in the nicest possible way?' Christina asked with a wry little smile, and Fiona nodded.

'He'll enjoy it, of course,' she said, 'eventually. But it'll be worth it just for that initial look of shock on his face.'

'You're right,' Christina said, grinning because her friend's wicked enthusiasm was infectious. 'What time? I'll be there. I wouldn't miss that for the world.'

The thought stayed with her over the next week and a half. Whenever she was feeling a bit over-stressed or tired, she thought of the look on Adam's face as he walked through that door and she wanted to burst out laughing.

She could remember quite a few practical jokes which he had pulled on them years ago, when she and Fiona had been too young and unimaginative to retaliate.

This would be a bit of delayed poetic justice.

She made a point of shopping very carefully for her outfit. Fiona hadn't mentioned numbers to her, but she had a feeling that it was going to be quite a big party. There would be all the glamorous people, well-known faces, and, much as she knew she couldn't compete with the likes of models, there was no reason why she shouldn't look her best. Nothing too startling, of course. Startling outfits only ever really looked good on women with startling looks. But something chic and subtle. Something that would blend into the background without being thoroughly boring and nondescript.

She ended up buying a black dress with a wide neckline edged with a collar of narrow black chiffon, which lovingly outlined her figure and made her feel reasonably attractive.

This, she thought that Saturday, as she eyed her reflection in the mirror, was only fair, since the outfit had cost the earth, and what was the point of spending a lot of money if you ended up feeling run-of-the-mill?

She was taking a taxi to Fiona's house, and she was under strict instructions to be there no later than seven-thirty.

'We've all got to be well hidden by the time he arrives at eight-thirty,' she had said. 'I've told him that I'm bringing Simon over because there's something terribly important that we need to discuss. Together, as a family.'

'That should work,' Christina had replied, amused. She tried to imagine Adam's cold fury at the thought of what such a discussion might mean.

The house, large as it was, was already bursting at the seams by the time she arrived an hour and a half later.

Fiona greeted her at the door, divested her of the small gift she had brought along, and made a rudimentary effort to introduce her to some of the faces. But she was no good at that sort of thing. She was too easily distracted, and after fifteen minutes Christina began circulating on her own, quite content to observe from the sidelines.

She had been right about one thing: there were lots of beautiful people there. Some she recognised from previous parties. The well-known faces tended to clump together, no doubt sharing similar experiences of being accosted by fans of one sort or another.

The less well-known ones seemed by far the most interesting, and over the next forty-five minutes she made a huge effort to introduce herself to them.

It was a technique which she had mastered over the years, even though she might be feeling scared stiff inside.

It was, in fact, one of the advantages of freelancing. It forced you to cultivate contacts, to brave the possible scorn, or boredom, of people whose business you wanted to court.

Now it was a talent that appeared to be standing her in good stead. She was chatting amicably with a journalist, who was there, he swore, socially and not on business, when Fiona announced, in a wildly theatrical voice, that it was time to turn off the lights and await Adam's imminent entrance.

A little ripple of laughter spread through the crowd as the rooms fell into darkness, and voices which had been booming a minute before became hushed and conspiratorial.

Now's his cue, Christina thought, to throw the whole thing into mad disarray by not appearing.

But he did. After ten minutes of increasingly restless silence they all heard his car swing into the drive, followed shortly by the sharp click of his footsteps up to the front door.

Christina grinned as his key was inserted. Then he was there, standing framed in the doorway, his black coat billowing around him because it was a freezing, windy evening.

She felt a little shiver run through her which she assumed must have been from the cold air blowing in, although she admitted that he did make an impressive sight, tall, lean and silhouetted quite starkly against the night skies, mesmerising, but dangerously so.

It was only a fleeting impression, because then the lights were switched on and everything was sudden chaos. The yelling of 'Happy birthday', the streamers, the guests crowding around him.

Christina watched from a distance. There was no way that she was going to get caught in the general stampede in his direction.

It was hard to tell what exactly was going through his head. She could see him distinctly, towering over most of the other people, his face a mask of politeness as he accepted their good wishes. Then he began making a path for himself through the crowds, a laborious process as he was continually stopped on the way.

Christina headed towards the kitchen, which had emptied on Adam's arrival and showed no signs of refilling.

It was cool there. She poured herself a drink of water from one of the dozens of bottles standing on the counter and stood for a while, staring out of the kitchen window.

She was hardly aware of the soft tread of footsteps behind her, and when he spoke into her ear she visibly started, spilling some of the water down her dress.

She turned around and made a great fuss of wiping it off, hardly daring to look into his face. It was funny, she had been as cool as a cucumber when he had walked through that front door, but now that he was standing right in front of her she was disgustingly nervous and apprehensive.

He was still in his suit, a deep grey hand-tailored one that emphasised the powerful lines of his body, although he had removed his tie and undone the first couple of buttons of his shirt. She could glimpse a tantalising sliver of muscular chest, and she quickly averted her eyes.

'Happy birthday, Adam,' she said huskily.

'"Happy" isn't quite the word I would use,' he replied. '"Happy" conjures up pictures of a meal in a restaurant, maybe the opera or the theatre. A surprise party definitely doesn't enter into the category of happy.'

He poured himself a gin and tonic and stood there drinking it, observing her over the rim of the glass.

'I expect you and Fiona are feeling terribly pleased with yourselves?'

'I don't know what you mean,' Christina protested feebly, and he raised his eyebrows expressively. There definitely was something dangerous about him, she decided, even without the startling backdrop and the billowing coat. It was there in the calculating glint in his eyes, the hard set of his mouth, the general impression of a man of formidable intellect and self-control.

'You know exactly what I mean. You always know exactly what I mean. It's simply that at times you choose to pretend that you don't. Another one of your odd little traits.'

Odd little traits? 'Thank you very much for making me sound like a creature from another planet,' she replied, not liking his observation. 'Shouldn't you be out there mingling with your guests? After all, we've been here for well over an hour waiting for your arrival.'

'I'm sure you have. With bated breath. Fiona knows I hate these sort of affairs, and I suspect you know it as well.' He swallowed the rest of his drink in one gulp and she suddenly wanted to laugh out loud. Poor little Adam, how nice to see him in an uncomfortable position just for once.

'I suspect I don't know what you're talking about,' she said, stifling her amusement, and his eyes narrowed on her, 'but I'm having a wonderful time, just in case you're interested.' The two glasses of wine, top-quality stuff and very drinkable, had gone to her head and she was feeling pleasantly warm towards the world.

'So it would seem. But is it because you're enjoying the party, or enjoying a quiet little laugh at my expense?'

'I'd never dream of laughing at you, Adam,' she said, working hard to appear serious. She moved towards the door, but before she could pull it open he was ahead of her, propping himself against the shut door with one hand, so that she had to stand there and face him.

'What a complex little creature you are,' he mocked. 'I'd forgotten until we had that little spell of enforced intimacy at the cottage in Scotland. Isn't it funny what you can rediscover about a person in a matter of a few days?'

His eyes wandered down to her lips, and she felt a jolt of alarm shoot through her.

She wasn't the game-playing type, and this smacked of something of a game to her. One played at her expense. Did he imagine that he could rattle her with that deliberately suggestive look in his eyes? She might be feeling light-headed from the drink, but she was far from feeling out of control. She knew and he knew that she wasn't his type, so all this intent charm was wasted on her.

'Isn't it,' she agreed coolly, transferring her attention away from his face to the door-handle. 'But I can stand only so much enforced intimacy with you in a lifetime, and I think my limit was used up at the cottage, so if you don't mind?'

His face hardened, and she felt a little jab of satisfaction. She didn't care what he thought of her, just so long as he didn't suspect that she was more vulnerable to his charm than she wanted to be.

'You're a cool customer, aren't you, Tina?' His voice was speculative. 'So self-contained. What happened between you and that Robinson chap? Under all that control, there's a fire burning, isn't there? I felt its heat for a brief while at the cottage. Did he discover that he couldn't handle you? Was that it?'

'I don't have to listen to this!' The roar in her heart was deafening.

He ignored her strangled protest. 'What did he do for you? Did you sleep with him? Were you in love with him?'

'That's none of your business.' She turned away, her voice barely audible. 'I don't pry into your life!' She raised her eyes to his, floundering in the unfathomable blue depths. 'I don't ask you about the women you've slept with!' she continued defiantly. 'What if I were in love with Greg?' she asked. 'He might have been everything you said, but you're hardly a shining example of what every woman wants, are you?'

'There are a lot of women who would disagree with you on that score,' he said, unperturbed by her fast-disappearing self-control, that wonderful self-control that had fuelled this conversation in the first place.

'And where are they?' Christina threw at him. 'I don't exactly see them queuing up to give glowing reports about you to their successors! If you're such an eligible candidate, how is it that you've never married? Or is eligibility synonymous with playing the field?'

'I play the field,' he answered with steel in his voice, 'because the alternative has never appealed. Marriage, from what I've seen, is an institution that leaves a lot to be desired.'

'Your parents were happy!'

'My parents were anything *but* happy. My father slept with a series of women. In fact he was such an avid womaniser that running the company eventually took a back seat to his affairs. Why do you think it was in such a mess when I took over after his death?'

Christina opened her mouth, but nothing came out.

'But,' she eventually stammered, 'they seemed...' Her voice trailed off as she saw the derisive curl of his lips.

'So they did. Not even Fiona suspected a thing. I suppose that's one thing I should be grateful for—that she, at any rate, was left with a few illusions. So you see, my dear Tina, as far as I'm concerned, commitment is a joke.'

They were staring at each other and she felt as though she were standing on the edge of a precipice, hardly daring to breathe in case she fell over.

'That still doesn't give you the right to treat women how you want,' she said eventually, her mind still reeling from his revelations.

'I treat women how they want to be treated, believe me.' He paused and gave her a long look, his blue eyes hooded and unreadable. 'When I touched you in the cottage, it was because you wanted to be touched, whether you deny it or not.'

There was a thick silence and Christina felt giddy with apprehension and nerves. She wanted desperately to push past him, to get away from the hypnotic gleam of his eyes, but her body was locked in a block of ice and she found that she was rooted to the spot.

'No!' she managed to protest, which made him laugh softly.

'Just as you want to be touched right now.' He raised his hand and trailed a lazy line along her collarbone, over the chiffony neckline, then along her breast, circling the nipple, which hardened under the light caress.

Then a wild, hot flush spread through her, jerking her into action. She stumbled back and at the same time the door was pushed by someone outside.

He released her, the door opened, and she escaped quickly back into the living-room, losing herself in the noise and crowds.

What was happening to her? she wondered, trembling. One minute everything in her life seemed to be ticking along nicely. Her job was satisfying. Her most tiresome problem had been the two corgis and their temperamental owner. But even that problem had only really aroused a certain amount of affectionate amusement.

Now a network of unexpected complications seemed to have cropped up all over the place. Her mind kept insisting on replaying images of Adam, memorising little details about him, adding those details to a reservoir of stored-up images which she had not even known, until now, that she possessed. And if that wasn't disturbing enough, she now found that her body had decided to turn traitor as well, responding to him with a hunger that made her head swim.

Back there, in the kitchen, he had touched her, lightly and expertly, to prove a point. He might not be prepared to offer commitment to the women he slept with, but that didn't mean that they didn't want him anyway. Except, she told herself with angry disgust, she wasn't one of his women and never would be, never would want to be.

She looked at him across the room, surrounded by a circle of friends, the majority of them women. He had his arm around one of them. She was tall, blonde and had that sort of drop-dead beauty that would make most heads swivel. Her hair was straight and short, her make-up understated, but not so understated as to give the impression of someone scrubbed clean. Of course she would be a model. Weren't they all? This was his type of woman. That thought slowly brought her back to earth and restored some of her shattered calm.

She caught Fiona's eye and watched as her friend weaved a way through the crowds and finally deposited herself on the stair next to her.

'A huge success,' Christina said, covering her confused thoughts with a grin. 'You should give lessons on throwing parties. You've managed just the right combination here of beautiful people, good music, good food and plenty of drink.'

Fiona pulled a face. 'I was hoping for more of an adverse reaction from Adam,' she said with a plaintive sigh, 'but he didn't even seem embarrassed by the whole thing.'

Christina's eyes drifted across to where he was standing. Was it her imagination or was the space between the blonde and him a little less than when she'd looked over a minute ago? If this continued they would fuse in about half an hour.

She dragged her eyes away, because the sight of it was producing a bitter taste in her mouth which she could only put down to disgust.

'I'm sure deep down he's furious,' Christina soothed, recalling their conversation in the kitchen.

'Really? He doesn't seem terribly furious from where I'm sitting.'

'No,' Christina agreed, and her voice was a shade cooler, 'he doesn't, does he? Who's his lady friend?' She hadn't wanted to ask that question. She hadn't wanted to betray any curiosity at all, but she couldn't seem to help herself. Her mouth framed the words independently of her brain and uttered them before she had time to think.

'Frances,' said Fiona, frowning, 'I think. I've only met her once. She's a model.'

'Oh, really? What a surprise.'

Fiona laughed and turned to her friend. 'He's always been attracted to the same type.'

'Maybe he finds women with brains a little too intimidating.'

'You could be right. Although he likes you and you have brains.'

Christina laughed shortly. She didn't want Adam Palmer to like her. 'Like' was such a nondescript word. It was what you felt about your next-door neighbour, or the butcher. Not that it mattered to her whether he liked, disliked or thoroughly detested her, she decided.

'He doesn't like me, Fiona,' she said, 'he tolerates me. The way you tolerate something unpleasant and inconvenient that you accidentally might bump into.'

'Like a traffic jam?' Fiona asked helpfully.

'That wasn't quite the metaphor I had in mind. But it doesn't matter. You know what I mean. Your brother puts up with my company when it's absolutely necessary. Not,' she added emphatically, 'that I mind in the slightest.' She laughed. 'I'm the same towards him.'

'Are you?' Fiona looked at her friend dubiously. 'You once had a crush on him.'

Good grief, Christina thought, had that been apparent to the entire universe, and was she destined to be reminded of it for the remainder of her life?

'Once,' she said, trying not to sound annoyed at this unwelcome reminder of her stupid youthful folly. 'Once. Once I wore my hair in pigtails. That doesn't mean that I still do so now, does it?'

Fiona looked at her blankly and said, 'You'd look cute in pigtails. Like a schoolgirl. You have such a young face.'

Christina was torn between a desire to laugh and one to groan aloud in frustration. Dear, sweet Fiona. How could Adam be so hard, so arrogant, so damned sharp, when his sister was so adorable and ingenuous? They were like chalk and cheese. No wonder he felt obliged to protect her for her own good. In the wrong hands, she could be putty.

'What I'm trying to say,' she murmured gently, 'is that I don't particularly care for your brother, and the feeling's mutual.'

'Is it?' Fiona thought that one over for a few seconds, then she said, 'If that's the case, then why does he want to employ you?'

Christina's eyes had been wandering around the room. It was fun watching the various stages of inebriation. She only hoped this crowd of people would be taking taxis back to their homes. Now, at Fiona's words, her attention returned sharply to her friend sitting on the stair next to her.

'What do you mean?' she asked tightly.

'He asked me all about your work. How much of it I'd seen. What your portfolio was like. He said that he wouldn't mind giving you a try at doing a cover for one of his magazines. He thinks the photographers they've been using have sunk into a rut. He said that something different might encourage sales to pick up. He has his team working on a fresh approach to the articles, and you... well, you're in line for redesigning the graphics.' Fiona looked rather pleased with herself for this extended speech.

'I don't need your brother's patronage,' Christina muttered through her teeth.

'I thought you were always on the look-out for freelance work.'

'I am,' she replied evenly, 'but I've got quite enough on my plate at the moment. So you can tell him that the next time he mentions that little idea of his.'

Fiona nodded agreeably enough. 'OK.'

'Fine.'

She looked across to where the blonde and Adam were still pressed against each other. He had his arm slung around her shoulder so that his hand fell lightly in front of her breast. A few inches closer and he would be caressing it. The thought sickened her. Why did they have to show that kind of intimacy in public? Couldn't they wait until they made it to the bedroom? It was in bad taste, she thought resentfully.

He looked across suddenly and caught her eyes on him, and he raised one eyebrow in question.

Christina scowled ill-humouredly at him and looked away.

If he thought, she decided, that he was going to have anything to do with her on a work basis, then he was in for a shock, because the last thing she would ever do was accept his hand-outs.

CHAPTER FIVE

IF CHRISTINA could honestly say to herself that he had not managed to ruffle her feathers, then there would be no reason why she should be worrying about hearing from him. But the fact was that she was doing just that.

Three days ago she had left his party with a brief little wave in his direction, hurrying out of the house just in case he took it into his head to come over and personally escort her through the front door.

And since then she had spent every waking moment in a state of nervous tension, wondering whether the next time she answered the phone his deep, velvety voice would be at the other end. Whenever she came home she would apprehensively switch on her answering machine, and hold her breath while the incoming calls were played back.

And, most of all, she had concocted a dozen different reasons why she would not, could not, possibly do any work for his publishing firm. She was overworked at the moment. She was coming down with something. She would be out of the country. She had no experience in that particular field. The excuses ran on and on in her brain until they made her dizzy.

Underneath them all there was only one reason why she would not accept work from him. She couldn't bear his proximity, and that was because she loathed him and, more than that, loathed the response he had drawn out of her for his own amusement. He was too attractive, too charming for his own good, and she wasn't even going to put herself in a position where she might forget, however briefly, the lessons she had learnt from Greg.

She propped her feet up on the footstool in front of her and cradled her mug in both her hands while her attention drifted away from the television programme which she had been watching, and chewed away at the tiring question of why Adam Palmer was disturbing the calm surface of her life so very much.

She thought of the blonde, Frances, and decided that that was just one more nail in his coffin as far as she was concerned. A womaniser. Weren't they the worst sort?

She tried to stifle the pang of sympathy she felt for him whenever she thought of how his father's infidelities must have affected him, changed him, no doubt, from a boy to a man. When had he found out? He hadn't said, but, thinking back, she could remember how quickly he seemed to have donned an air of cynicism, which at the time she had found wildly exciting.

Sympathy, though, was the last thing she should feel for him, she thought. All said and done, she would have to be ultra-careful when and if she happened to bump into him again. There was no use pretending that he hadn't aroused feelings of desire in her, and she would have to make sure that she didn't succumb to that seductive charm of his, if he ever took it into his head to use it on her again.

Reason, though, was on her side, because he wasn't attracted to her. Despite the fact that recently she had been paying a lot more attention to that reflection that stared back at her from the mirror, she would be a fool to develop a convenient blind eye to her own physical shortcomings. Greg's words kept coming back to her, making her head swim.

Of course, Adam Palmer was to blame for that. She didn't care what he thought of her physically, but there was something in his expert appraisal of her which made her look at herself and find herself wanting. Those cool blue eyes could evaluate a woman and dismiss her in a matter of seconds, even though to all intents and purposes he was as charming as the devil himself to everyone.

She had always known that to be a trait of his.

He was one of those men, she had long ago decided, who was attracted to the decorative type of woman. He dealt with the intellectuals on a business level. Perhaps he didn't want his private life cluttered with them as well. He got enough mental stimulation at work. He wanted to relax in the company of a woman who perhaps excited him physically, but didn't tax his mind too much.

Why was this whole thing bothering her so much? she wondered irritably. She didn't want to think about the wretched man. That was a bad habit which she thought she had put well and truly behind her years ago. Now she had enough on her plate to occupy her mind without Adam Palmer cropping up like a bad penny every two minutes.

She was staring at the television set, frowning, trying to work out what had happened in the last ten minutes, when the telephone rang from just beside her, and she automatically lifted the receiver, and absent-mindedly said, 'Yes?'

'Tina. Have I caught you in the middle of something?'

Christina sat up straight, her nerve-ends tingling as Adam's sexy deep voice reached her.

'Yes,' she lied, 'I was in the middle of some work.'

'Were you?' he asked politely. 'Well, this won't take long.'

Most men, she wanted to point out, would have done the decent thing and suggested that they call back later. Why not you?

'I don't think I've seen you since your birthday party,' she said, buying time and talking off the top of her head in an attempt to gather her thoughts together. 'It was very enjoyable. Did you enjoy yourself? I'm sorry I didn't manage to catch you before I left.'

'Yes, yes, it was very enjoyable,' Adam said with a trace of impatience in his voice, 'And I'm quite sorry you didn't catch me as well, because I wanted to talk to you about this little project I want you to do for my company. I would have contacted you sooner, but I've been out of the country for the past two days on business.'

She heard him take a sip of a drink and the faint tinkle of ice in a glass, and she had a very vivid picture of him sitting in that den of his, his eyes half closed as he tilted his head back and swallowed some whisky and soda, his long legs stretched out in front of him. In the semi-darkness of the den, he would look even more dark and brooding than he normally did.

The image was so frighteningly real that she had to blink it away.

'Anywhere nice?' she asked.

'Paris. When can I see your portfolio?'

'Ah,' she said, 'I'm afraid there are a few problems on that front. I haven't got it at the moment. I've lent it out to one of my clients.'

'Who? I'll get my courier to pick it up first thing in the morning.'

This is ridiculous, Christina thought wildly. Why don't I just accept this damned job and carry on as normal? Chances were she wouldn't even see him on any of her shoots. He was the top man, hardly likely to be swanning around watching her take photographs. Besides, she could hardly expect to continue avoiding him for the rest of her life, simply because, for some inexplicable reason, she was finding his presence unsettling.

'No, no,' she said hastily, 'that won't be necessary. Look, Adam, there's no need for you to feel obliged to offer me any freelance work with your company. I——'

'I've never felt obliged to do anything in my life before,' he cut in bluntly, 'and I don't intend to start now. Now when can I see this portfolio of yours?'

'Well——' Christina said feebly, and he interrupted in the sort of voice that made her feel as though he was doing her a favour by agreeing to meet her, when it was the other way around.

'What about tomorrow for lunch? I'm free between eleven-thirty and two. That should give you ample opportunity to collect this portfolio of yours from wherever it is.'

'Yes, but——'

'Shall we say twelve-thirty at the . . . ?' and he said the name of one of London's more exclusive restaurants.

'Fine,' Christina said in a strangled voice, and she heard the click of the receiver as he hung up.

She felt as though she had been mown down by a car. Was he always as forceful as this in his dealings with people, or did he save some modicum of good manners for other, more worthwhile individuals?

She spent an inordinate length of time the following day reviewing her portfolio. It was a good one. She knew that without any lack of modesty. She had perfected a natural talent and honed it into something quite impressive.

As far as she could see, it had been good luck that she had been able to turn something she loved doing into a job. Not many people had that opportunity.

The photographs in her portfolio ranged from evocative black and white portraits to crisp colour photos of everything from children to buildings.

She zipped up the leather case and spent the next hour dressing very carefully. There was no sense in trying to emphasise her femininity. He would take one look at her efforts and throw her one of those amused little smiles he specialised in. And besides, that wasn't her style. She preferred clothes that were functional and comfortable. For interviews with prospective clients she invariably wore a suit.

Now she pulled out a camel-coloured one. The skirt fitted her to the knees and the jacket was a boxy, Chanel-type one with a rounded neck and buttons down the front. It was unobtrusive and businesslike and she felt rather pleased as she studied herself in the full-length mirror.

All she needed, she thought drily, was a pair of spectacles, and she would fit the role of the sexless career girl down to the last button on her jacket.

She arrived at the restaurant exactly on time. Punctuality was a virtue she cherished highly, having been kept waiting more than once by late clients. To be late, as far as she was concerned, wasn't the privilege of a woman, but just downright rude.

Adam, she was pleased to see, was already there. She was shown to his table and he half stood as she approached.

'You're on time,' he said without preamble. 'That's good. I like that in a person.' He signalled to one of the waiters, who came over to take her order for an aperitif, and as she asked for a glass of mineral water with a slice of lemon she could feel him watching her. It made her skin tingle.

She wasn't about to let him throw her out of joint, though. She was here on business and when it came to that area she was poised and self-confident and totally in control.

She had brushed her hair back into a neat chignon, which she considered made her appear even more sexless; then she told herself off for even thinking about how she looked at all.

She smiled at him and said briskly, 'Would you like to tell me exactly what sort of job you have in mind for me?'

'No preliminary small talk?'

'We could, if you like. What would you like to small-talk about? The weather? Your party? The state of the economy?'

The waiter brought them their menus and she busied herself looking at it, already knowing what she intended to have, but taking her time perusing the dishes listed because it meant that she didn't have to look at him.

He looked devastating. His dark hair had been combed back and the muted colours of his suit lent his dark good looks even more sex appeal.

'The hard-headed businesswoman to the core,' he said lazily, shutting his menu with a little snap. 'You can step down from there, Tina. Don't forget that we know each other. You don't have to impress me.'

Christina closed her menu and regarded him evenly.

'I wasn't trying to impress you. I'm here on business. I just thought that we might as well get it out of the way.'

'Before we move on to what?'

Was there a teasing note in his voice or was it her imagination? Certainly she got the impression that he was laughing at her and her carefully groomed image, and that made her angry.

'Before you move into a taxi to carry you back to your office, and I head home to continue my work.'

The waiter came to take their order and she looked at Adam from under her lashes, absorbing the strong lines of his face.

'Have you spoken to Fiona recently?' he asked, leaning forward and resting both elbows on the table.

Christina shook her head. 'No, why? Please don't tell me that you have any more problems with her and that you need to enlist my help, because you can count me out.'

He laughed softly. 'Nothing like that. Not at the moment, anyway. No, she's found another man. Or rather I have.'

'What do you mean?' Christina asked, puzzled.

'I've decided, in the wake of her last disastrous love-affair, that I should find someone suitable for her, since she shows no sign of doing so herself. So I introduced her to a friend and business acquaintance of mine, Terry White. I am reliably informed by the opposite sex that he's a good catch, and Fiona, thankfully, seems to share my opinion.'

'Good grief,' Christina said, forgetting about her cool image, 'that has to be just about the most arrogant thing I've ever heard in my entire life.'

Adam looked back at her, unperturbed. 'Fiona seems happy enough with the arrangement.'

'Or that's what you'd like to believe, at any rate.'

'On that soapbox of yours again, Tina?' His mouth hardened fractionally. 'You always were one to jump up and down for a cause and conveniently forget about reality.'

'That's not true!'

'Don't you think that common interests and similar goals in life can bind two people together far more than lust? Terry and Fiona are ideally suited. And they seem attracted enough to one another. So where's the problem?'

'The problem is your mania for running other people's lives!'

He shrugged. 'I'm protective of my sister. As for the rest of the world, they're quite welcome to run their own little lives. I don't try and interfere in yours, do I?'

'And how would you do that?' Christina retorted heatedly.

'For a start I'd strip you of that severe suit you're wearing. I'd also get you to stop being so damned defensive towards the opposite sex. Greg Robinson isn't worth that sort of legacy.'

'Any more observations?' She could hardly speak coherently. 'Thank you, but I like the way I am, just in case it matters! I can just imagine the sort of vacant, platinum-dyed blonde you'd turn me into!'

'Don't be stupid.'

'I'm not! You talk about Fiona and Terry, a relationship based on mutual similarities. How would you know? Your relationships are all based on lust! You practically admitted as much to me! And if I were in any doubt, I saw you at your party with that blonde draped over you like a second skin!'

She wished the ground would open up and swallow her. She hadn't meant that to slip out.

'Oh, you did, did you?' Adam asked, the corners of his lips twitching. 'And naturally you assumed that we do nothing in our spare time but make love, and that there's absolutely nothing between her ears but stuffing?'

'I didn't assume anything of the sort,' Christina said awkwardly, 'though she is a model, isn't she?'

'She's also an English graduate.'

'Oh.' A wave of colour flooded her cheeks. So maybe she had jumped to a few wrong conclusions. Unfortunately that didn't make her feel in the slightest bit better. She preferred her misconception that the blonde was brainless.

'Very chauvinistic of you to assume that because Frances is blonde and beautiful she can't possibly be bright.' He smiled at her and she wanted to knock his complacent front teeth out.

She concentrated on the remnants of the food on her plate, relieved when the waiter provided a distraction by clearing away their plates, and then, a few minutes later, reappearing with two cups and a jug of percolated coffee.

'We don't seem to have discussed business at all,' she said stiffly. 'Shall I pour you some coffee?'

He nodded and she poured him out a cup and listened while he began explaining exactly what he wanted from her. The cover shot for the magazine would be, as luck would have it, Frances, and he wanted something unusual and eye-catching to be done.

'Nothing run-of-the-mill,' he said. 'I'm fed up with pretty girls staring out at me from the magazine racks in newsagents. I want something different.'

'What about doing away with the model altogether?' Christina asked. 'You could take the picture from one of your lead features in the magazine.'

He nodded, giving it some thought. Then he said she would have to do some shots, purely fashion-based, for the glossy centre pictures, and she nodded. This was fairly familiar ground. She had worked with models before for two magazines, neither of which was part of Adam's publishing house, and had found the work simple enough if a little tedious. Her attention tended to stray.

'Can I take your portfolio with me?' he asked, as he drained his coffee-cup and looked at his watch.

Time for my dismissal, she thought wryly.

'I make a point of never lending it out,' she said automatically, and he frowned at her.

'Really? I thought your precious portfolio had only this morning been rescued from a client?'

Christina felt her cheeks go pink. 'Oh, yes, he was an exception,' she said hastily.

'Was he?' Adam looked at her curiously. 'Why?'

'He's an old friend,' she mumbled, off the cuff. 'I often do him favours. I've known him a long time. He puts quite a bit of business my way.'

She dwindled off into silence and wondered why she was gibbering on with some fictitious excuse for something that was none of his business after all.

'You often do him favours?' He stood up and she followed suit, preceding him to the cloakroom, where he reached for her coat and helped her into it, an awkward exercise which was not helped by the fact that her body was stiff as a board in an attempt to avoid any physical contact with him.

'What sort of favours?' he continued, interestedly. 'And I naïvely assumed that Robinson was the only man in your life for some time.'

Why? she thought. Because I'm plain? Not the sort to be surrounded by a bevy of suitors? A few weeks ago that thought would never have occurred to her—her inherent sense of self-worth wouldn't have allowed it—and it annoyed her to think that Adam Palmer had chiselled open chinks which had formerly not existed.

'Thank you for the lunch,' she said, dodging his question. 'When do you want me to meet you so that we can take care of the details?'

They were in the road now, and he reached out to hail a taxi, which swerved across to stop in front of them. He leaned in and gave the taxi driver her home address, then he opened the door for her to enter. She slipped past him quickly.

'Contact my personnel officer tomorrow,' he told her, slamming shut the door and leaning down to look in at her. 'She'll have the contract ready.'

The wind whipped his hair across his forehead and he raked his fingers through it, a casual, unthinking gesture to which she found she was paying an abnormal amount of attention.

'What will you tell your regular photographer?' she asked, dragging her eyes away, and he shrugged.

'That someone else is being brought in to try and provide a change. What else? I don't intend to beat around the bush on this one. I don't believe in carrying dead wood. I'm hoping that he'll derive some inspiration from you, in which case things will carry on as normal next month, but, if I find that he's become a liability in my organisation, then...'

He let his comment hang unfinished in the air, and Christina shivered. In the tough world of business, there was no room for people who didn't contribute their way, but it was still a little alarming to see such ruthless power in action.

Adam Palmer, she realised, was not a man to overlook incompetence out of politeness. He would seek to eliminate it.

'Then you'll liquidate him,' she finished, and he gave her a cool smile.

'I'm not a member of the Mafia. No, he would be financially taken care of, perhaps moved to another department, or sent on some kind of refresher training course. It's a problem to be faced when and if it arises.'

He slammed shut the door, and gave her a little farewell salute, and the taxi slowly eased its way into the London traffic.

She sat back and stared vacantly out of the window, but her thoughts were elsewhere. It had been a profitable meeting, that much she couldn't deny. To be able to quote Adam Palmer's publishing house on her CV would be a feather in her cap. His organisation was massive, highly profitable and extremely well respected. She tried to remember what it had been like when his father was alive, whether in retrospect she could see the tell-tale signs of its gradual failure, but she couldn't. She had been too young then to pay much attention to such far-off things as companies and their profitability. Little wonder that Fiona had never suspected anything remiss in her parents' relationship, and Adam was right to withhold the knowledge from her. She was surprised that he had said anything to *her* about it, but maybe it had been meant to put her in her place rather than as a show of confidence. She dragged her thoughts back to the present.

She had not wanted to accept any sort of job from Adam, but she could see now that any ideas that she might have had about being patronised had been way off course.

In fact she was surprised that that thought could ever have entered her mind. He was simply not the sort to patronise. If he had looked at her portfolio and had been unimpressed, she would be sitting here right now without his lucrative offer ringing in her ears.

Because lucrative it most certainly was. The fee he had mentioned was sizeable, far more than she had been paid by the other magazines she had worked for. And the job was not one which was going to cause her undue anxiety. He had left with her suggestion that the cover represent an aspect of one of the articles rather than another attractive face, and no doubt his decision would be waiting for her in the capable hands of his personnel officer to be imparted when they met the following day.

And that, she thought, would be the end of his involvement with her on this job. She would now be working with a variety of other people, all cogs in the vast wheel that made his organisation run smoothly.

Her spirits were still wonderfully buoyant the following morning when she knocked on the door of the personnel officer.

She had visited Adam's headquarters only once before, a long time previously when she had arranged to meet Fiona for lunch and was picking her up there. It had not changed very much. It was still an impressive building, not massively large, but with that clinical elegance that often underlay a well-run organisation.

The minute you stepped through the glass doors into the foyer, you had the impression that this was a place where things got done.

She suspected that even the plants would have been coerced into some job or other if Adam had had his way.

A woman's voice called her in, and Christina pushed open the wooden door and stepped into a plush room dominated by a huge desk, behind which sat a woman in her mid-thirties, in a dark suit and with a friendly but efficient face.

The perfect corporate look, Christina thought with a trace of amusement. Well, at least he did not discriminate against women when it came to his employees. The woman sitting behind the desk with the amicable, shrewd smile on her face was in a very senior position indeed.

Christina accepted the outstretched hand, but before she could sit down the other woman, who insisted on being called Mallory, said without preamble, 'Before you make yourself comfortable, I might as well tell you that Mr Palmer has asked me to send you up to him as soon as I've given you your contract.' She handed over some official pieces of paper, and Christina accepted them with a puzzled frown.

'Whatever for?'

'I presume he wants to discuss a few last-minute details of your job with you.' She shrugged and smiled with genuine warmth. 'I'm sure it's important. He rarely does anything without a very good reason.'

'I'm sure,' Christina said, returning her smile with a wry one of her own. She flicked through the document in her hand, which looked straightforward enough, a variation on the many which she had seen and signed ever since she had begun work on a freelance basis.

'I'll show you up to his office,' Mallory said, moving around and walking briskly to the door. 'He hates being kept waiting. It's one of the very first things I always tell new employees.'

What are the other things? Christina wanted to know. A few other essential ground rules to avoid antagonising the big man?

They walked towards the lift, and as it whisked them up to the other floor Mallory asked about Christina's line of work, keeping up an easy banter until they reached the outer office, where his secretary was busily inputting information into a word processor.

She raised her eyes for a fraction as they entered and nodded at Mallory.

'I'll leave you here,' Mallory said, shaking her hand firmly. 'See you soon.'

Then she was gone, and the secretary, a middle-aged woman with a grim set to her features, knocked sharply on the adjoining door to his office.

Christina looked around her. This was unexpected. She felt nervous and taken aback at the prospect of meeting Adam yet again. It seemed that ever since he had burst into her flat on his mad chase after Fiona she had been thrown into his company far too much for her liking.

Now she smoothed her skirt and composed her face as his secretary stood back to allow her entry into his office.

It was huge. The speckled blue of the wallpaper, combined with the very dark wood of the furniture, gave it a peculiarly masculine look. Apart from that, though, there was nothing to indicate what sort of person sat behind the desk, except that it was obviously one who wielded a great deal of power.

No photos on the desk, one very functional plant in the corner, and only one picture on the wall, a vaguely abstract affair that gave no indication of what it was meant to represent.

She would have expected the walls to be lined with framed covers of his magazines, but perhaps he didn't care for dozens of women's faces staring out at him every minute of the day.

'Will that be all, sir?' the secretary asked from behind Christina's back, and Adam nodded, before returning his attention to Christina.

He nodded to the chair facing him, an oddly masculine gesture, and she sat down tentatively.

'Well, what do you think?' he asked, and she looked at him, bewildered.

'About what?'

'The office.' He gave a broad gesture. 'I saw you looking at it with an expression of disapproval on your face.'

'Was I?' She stared at him, startled.

'You were,' he said drily. 'You have a remarkably expressive face, even though you try so hard to conceal it.'

That made her blush, something she hated doing in his presence because it made her feel vulnerable.

'I was thinking,' she responded with deliberate calm, 'that this office doesn't give anything away about you. Anyone could work here, sit at that desk.'

'And what's wrong with that?' he asked, vaguely amused. 'Surely you don't believe that the working area should be cluttered with little stuffed mascots and photos of every member of my family?'

'I guess not.'

'They're unnecessary distractions,' he said, tapping his fountain-pen on the polished wood of his desk. 'Although,' he continued, as if slightly surprised by the thought that had come to his head, 'the real distractions exist in the mind and not on celluloid.'

'I presume that that's a reference to Frances of the English degree?' Christina said politely, her insides churning at the thought of the other woman possessing the power to distract him, and he gave her a curious look.

'Who else?' he asked rhetorically. 'Anyway, moving on to the matter in hand...'

'Yes,' she said crisply, 'the matter in hand. I'm surprised you asked to see me. I thought that we had ironed out quite a few of the details over lunch yesterday.'

'Quite a few of them,' Adam agreed smoothly. 'There are just one or two things which I wanted to discuss with you personally. The first is that I've given some thought

to what you said about shooting a cover to feature one
of the highlights in the magazine.'

'And?'

'And I think it's a very good idea.' He gave her a dry
smile. 'No need to look so surprised. I can pay the oc-
casional compliment.'

I'm sure, Christina thought, but not to me.

'So you want to brief me on what I'll be
photographing,' she said.

He looked at her from under his lashes. 'And where,'
he said silkily.

She didn't like that expression on his face. It made
her wary.

'You have a passport, I take it?' he said, and she
nodded.

'Good, because we're running an article on carnivals
around the world, and as of next week you'll be in
Trinidad. I hope,' he added, 'you won't find that
too inconvenient.'

CHAPTER SIX

CHRISTINA sat down and looked at him blankly.

'Trinidad,' she said. 'Isn't that somewhere in the West Indies? Where, right now, there's lots of sunshine?'

He nodded and she eyed him warily. 'Why me? Why not someone more experienced? You've never used me before. How do you know that sending me won't be a waste of your money?'

'Oh, for God's sake,' he snapped irritably, and she could see that her reaction was getting on his nerves, 'do you usually try and dissuade your clients from using your services?'

'Of course not . . .'

'Then why the string of questions? If I didn't want to hire you, believe me, you wouldn't be sitting where you are now. And as for not knowing your work—I've seen your portfolio. Not,' he continued, standing up and moving across to the window to stare down, his profile to her, 'that that was the persuading factor in my hiring you. I'm usually good at judging people, and I trust you to do your job well.'

'I'm flattered,' Christina said, wondering whether she should be pleased at that compliment or offended by the image it conjured up of her as predictable and efficient and ever so boring. 'I had no idea that business tycoons operated on instinct.'

He turned to face her, his arms folded across his chest, and with the cold, bright sun behind him there was something crazily attractive about him. Her heart began to beat a little harder, although the expression on her face didn't change.

'Instinct got me where I am today,' he said without warmth. 'As I said, my father's company was dying on its feet when I found myself thrown in at the deep end. Bad management, bad investments—you name it. I had had no idea how bad it all was, because at the time I had been abroad for quite a while.'

'Would you have returned to England if you had known?' she asked.

'Oh, no.' He gave her a bitter, twisted smile. 'I couldn't stomach what was going on between my parents. I certainly wouldn't have felt inclined to bail the old man out of the mess he'd got himself into.'

'You mean that you ended up doing it for your sister...'

'And in the process I discovered that power and success bring their own rewards.'

'You mean the flocks of women?'

'If I didn't know better, I would have said that you were obsessed with my love-life.' He gave her a lingering, mocking stare that made her flush.

'You'd be wrong.'

He didn't comment on that and she was left wondering whether he believed her or not. Why couldn't she be cooler, more controlled in his presence? The thought of her silly blushes and embarrassed blunders made her wince. There was nothing appealing or attractive about an undesirable woman acting the coy teenager in the presence of a man like Adam. At the very least it was pathetic. She raised her chin, looked him straight in the eye, and said calmly, 'Now, moving on to the matter in hand...' She looked at her watch. 'I have a few appointments to keep, so...'

'Of course,' he murmured, over-seriously. 'You leave in three days' time. That should get you there with a couple of days to spare before the carnival begins. You'll be there for two weeks exactly—time to familiarise yourself, do your shoots, and then wind up with a few beach shots of the models for the centre pages. And, lastly, you'll be staying at the Hilton, right in the heart of things. Any questions?'

'I shall have to reschedule some of my engagements,' she said, half to herself, and he frowned.

'Yes, you will,' he agreed smoothly, 'because the time factor here is non-negotiable.'

'Would it have been negotiable if it weren't for the carnival?' she asked casually.

'No.'

'Because you're the boss and what you say goes, take it or leave it?'

'That's right.'

Behind those arrogant good looks, those peculiar, vivid blue eyes, she could see the ruthless businessman. In and out of work, she doubted that anything would be negotiable with him.

They briefly went over a few details and then the telephone rang and she rose to leave, looking at him hesitantly, wondering whether there was anything else he wanted to tell her, but there clearly wasn't. He waved to her in a gesture that implied that her time was up, but he wasn't even looking in her direction. His mind was now elsewhere, totally absorbed in whatever was being said to him down the line.

Christina quietly let herself out of his office, pausing on the way out as his secretary confirmed what he had already told her about collecting the itinerary.

She had greeted his proposition unenthusiastically, but later on she began to feel a little spark of excitement. Adam might have employed her, but he wouldn't be there in Trinidad with her. She would be able to do her own thing, without having to fight that stupid, breathless feeling that seemed to overwhelm her whenever he was around, and what could be more thrilling than a fortnight in Trinidad for the carnival?

She surveyed her wardrobe and then, in a fit of childish glee, she dragged down her suitcase from the top of her wardrobe and began filling it with enough light clothes to last two weeks. There wasn't a great deal. Some cotton tops and shorts, a couple of dresses, her entire collection of bathing-suits, which amounted to three, and a handful of outfits which she hoped would take her through any night-time affairs. She knew from experience that the crew who worked on shoots tended to be light-hearted and extrovert, the sort who could dig out excitement in the middle of a barren desert. So she very much doubted there would be too many evenings in on her own.

Then the models would be there as well, however many of them Adam decided to use. They probably wouldn't be a bundle of laughs. In their profession they couldn't afford too much humour. Bad for the facial lines.

There you go, she told herself severely, being a bitch again. Let's not forget the blonde bombshell with the brains to match.

She thought of Frances and decided that she would much sooner forget everything about the blonde bombshell with the brains to match.

The next two days flew past. She finalised a few of her jobs, ran around the shops madly trying to get herself a few more presentable outfits, which, in the depth of frozen February, was extremely difficult, and also telephoned Fiona, who confessed, rather sheepishly, that yes, she was seeing one of her brother's friends, and yes, he really was rather nice, not at all like some of the guys she had dated in the past.

Was it any wonder, Christina thought, that Adam Palmer waltzed through life so damned confidently? The whole world seemed destined to jump to his tune.

On the day that she left England it chose to snow— a light flurry which, the weather forecasters predicted with a hint of amazement in their voices, would prelude the start of some unusually wintry conditions.

At the airport, the crew of six who were accompanying her, one of whom she had coincidentally met a few months earlier on one of her jobs, spent a good while crowing about their good fortune.

Four men and two women, they were, as she had expected, outgoing and sociable and immediately included her in their group.

'Just think,' Harry, one of the lighting men, laughed, 'we'll be missing all the thrills of trains brought to a standstill because of frozen tracks and cars that suddenly decide that it's time to catch flu.'

Christina grinned and looked around the assorted group. They comprised the basic back-up team for a shoot, the minimal number of people, with only a few more due to arrive a few days later, including the models and their entourage.

'Adam's keeping the numbers down,' one of the girls explained to her on the flight across. 'He's not a great believer in wasting money on fifteen when half that number could do the job just as well.'

'Very sensible,' Christina agreed, looking at the girl sitting alongside her. She was tiny, with flaming red hair and a sweet face that always seemed to be smiling even when she was serious.

'Very. Hence the economy seats. He never flies first-class himself either,' she carried on with admiration in her voice. 'Isn't that great?'

'Amazing,' Christina said. 'What a paragon of virtue.'

There was no doubt that Adam Palmer inspired a great deal of loyalty and respect in his employees, if this cross-section of people was anything to go by. She found herself wondering whether his high-handed attitude was reserved specifically for her. From the looks of it, it certainly seemed that way.

It was a long flight, stopping at Barbados, and finally landing at Piarco Airport in Trinidad at a little after five in the afternoon.

Outside the aeroplane the atmosphere was steamy, and Christina immediately rolled up the sleeves of her cotton shirt as far as was possible. Even so, she was literally sweating by the time they made it into the airport terminal, which, thankfully, was air-conditioned.

'I think I was born for this climate!' Jennifer, her companion during the flight, announced. 'Shame I won't be able to tan, with my hair.'

Christina laughed. She found it quite easy to tan. It was one of the good things about her somewhat sallow complexion.

Around her was a hive of activity. She had known beforehand that this was a very popular time of the year for tourists, but she was amazed at the numbers of people swarming around the carousel, joining the queue through Customs.

Outside, two taxis were waiting to take them to their hotel, and she felt a little spurt of racing excitement.

How could she have ever balked at the prospect of being offered some freelance work by Adam? She must have been crazy.

As the taxis lazily manoeuvred the highway into the city centre, she gazed around her at the lushness of the vegetation, at the stalls filled with over-bright fruit that dotted the sides of the roads. She felt as though any minute she would blink and be back in her flat in

England, wondering how many layers of clothing she needed before she ventured outside.

Two days later, she decided that it would be very easy to become accustomed to the slow pace of this sort of lifestyle.

Adam's idea to get them there with enough time to explore before the carnival started in earnest had been a good one. It gave them all an opportunity to submerge themselves in the atmosphere of the place, a barely contained feverish excitement which infected them all and made their reactions to everything around them less inhibited.

She flexed her muscles on some shots that attempted to capture some of this sense of anticipation, but she was saving herself for the big event, two days when the nation would take to the streets in an orgy of music and dancing. The ultimate in masquerades.

And she knew the rest of the crew felt the same way.

They made exploratory trips to a couple of the beaches, with the assistance of one of Adam's contacts on the island, who acted as their guide, sizing up possible backdrops for the shoots of the models in a few days' time.

And by nightfall they all trooped back to the hotel, bone-weary. The heat had a way of sapping your energy. It had you up with the larks in the morning, but by nine at night you felt as though you could fall into bed and sleep for a hundred years.

Not that there was much chance of that. Their guide, a Trinidadian who insisted that they see as much as they could by night as well as by day, showed them all the spots where things were happening: the tents where the calypsonians competed, and the savannah where the kings and queens of the bands vied with each other for winning titles. And everywhere, by day and by night, on every radio in every possible place, there was the sound of the steel-bands, bursting into the air with a beat that made you want to jump up and dance.

Christina had never experienced anything like it before.

On the weekend before the carnival was due to begin the two models were due to arrive with their entourage.

'They'll probably be immune to what's happening over here,' Jennifer confided in her. 'They see so much that they become blasé after a while.'

Christina pictured Frances's exquisite face and she could see Jennifer's point. There was a look of boredom beneath those perfect features, which probably only became animated in front of a camera lens.

They were lounging by the pool, like lizards cooling themselves from the heat of the sun. Jennifer was wearing a huge hat that threw her face into shadow, but Christina was happily supine on a deckchair.

She felt wonderfully desultory. This was hardly like work at all. It was like a paid holiday. If she had the energy, she would probably feel guilty, but she hadn't.

She was feeling healthier, more vibrant than she had in a long time.

Her tan was coming along nicely, and the sun had managed to do the impossible—make her hair look alive. It had brought out the reds and golds beneath the dull browns. She was quite pleased with the overall effect.

Next to her, Jennifer was reading bits and pieces from a tourist guide which they had picked up in the hotel. Christina was half listening, half thinking about how she would angle some of her shots the following day.

She had already taken quite a few pictures of the kings and queens of the bands, magnificent structures that towered above the little people supporting them, and which depicted an array of themes designed to haunt the imagination.

Her eyes were closed, hidden behind a pair of dark sunglasses.

She was so completely relaxed that the sound of Adam's voice above her made her eyes jerk open with shock. For the most fleeting of seconds, as her eyes adjusted to the dazzling sun, she thought that she must have imagined it. But no such luck. She couldn't mistake that face anywhere.

He was standing next to her deckchair in a pair of pale green trousers and a shirt opened at the neck.

The blue eyes flickered over her as she propped herself into a sitting position, flushed with embarrassment.

Next to her Jennifer had stopped reading and was enthusiastically talking to him, while his eyes hovered between the two of them, giving Christina very little opportunity to compose herself.

She could hear her heart hammering away in her chest. If only she could drag her towel around her... But she knew that any such action would bring that awful suppressed grin of amusement to his lips.

So she remained as she was, half sitting, half lying, acutely conscious of the brevity of her bikini, two black strips of cloth that had somehow assumed the proportions of a handkerchief.

After what seemed like years of highly uncomfortable small talk, none of which Christina managed to take in, Jennifer was dismissed in that charming manner of his, and Christina watched in horror as her friend gathered up her belongings and headed towards the hotel.

Adam perched himself on the edge of the deckchair and gave her a long, lazy look.

'So,' he said, 'how are you enjoying Trinidad?'

'It's lovely,' Christina said, dismayed, thinking that she had been enjoying it a whole lot more than she would be from now on. 'What are you doing over here?' she asked as casually as she could, hoping she didn't sound as tense and apprehensive as she was feeling. 'I had no idea that you travelled the world every time there was a shoot for one of your magazines.' The polite enquiry emerged tinged with anxious accusation.

'I don't,' he replied smoothly, and if he had caught the tone in her voice he chose to ignore it.

'Then why are you here?' she asked bluntly, not caring at this point what he thought.

'You sound worried at my presence over here. Are you?'

'No. Why should I be?' She attempted some light laughter, which emerged more like a choking sound.

'How are you getting along with the team?' he asked casually, but before she could answer he continued, 'No, no need to reply. From the two I've spoken to, you're all getting along swimmingly.' The vivid blue eyes raked over her and he said flatly, 'I hope that in between this wonderful social life you're actually managing to remember that you're over here to work.'

Christina looked at him indignantly. 'Of course I'm remembering what I'm over here to do! You needn't worry that you won't get value for your money! Is that why you're over here? So that you can check up on me?'

'You over-estimate yourself. I have better things to do than fly halfway across the world to check up on you.'

His derisory reply brought a flush to her cheeks and she stared stubbornly ahead of her, at the pool.

'It just seems strange that you're over here,' she persisted, and his mouth hardened.

'It doesn't seem strange to anyone else. It pays to sometimes be out there, in the field, seeing what's happening first-hand. Delegation can end up by imprisoning you in an ivory tower, cut off from the lifeline of your company.'

'In that case, I do apologise and stand corrected.'

He gave her a long, hard look and then said coldly, 'I don't like that tone of voice. I'm your boss and you'll address me accordingly. The fact that we know each other is irrelevant.'

A faint pink colour stole up her cheeks. 'I resent your implication that I would take advantage of being out here to enjoy myself and overlook the fact that I'm being paid to do a job. I bet you don't run around levelling those sorts of accusations at your other employees.'

She was keeping her voice low and controlled as well, but she didn't feel at all controlled. She felt hot and flustered.

'I know the dedication of my other employees,' he said coolly, 'but, as you so eloquently reminded me, you're an unknown quantity. I have your portfolio to go on and my sister's enthusiastic recommendation.'

'I never asked for this job.'

'I'm aware of that and, despite what you think, I wasn't implying anything. I was merely laying down a few ground rules.'

His eyes flickered over her semi-clad body, and she felt a peculiar *frisson* ripple through her.

'I can't imagine why you'd feel the need to do that,' she pursued stubbornly, knowing that she ought just to let the matter drop.

'Well, you don't look terribly overworked at the moment,' he drawled smoothly. 'In fact I'd say that you've been spending quite a bit of time around the pool if that golden colour is anything to go by.'

There was a brief, lazy interest in his eyes and that made her angry. Did he imagine that she would giggle girlishly at this point and bat her eyelashes at him? She might look more appealing with a tan, but she was nothing compared to the Franceses of this world, and she resented his patronising imitation of flattery.

'Well you'd be wrong,' she said flatly, dragging the towel around her and not giving a damn what he thought. 'This is the second time I've been by this pool. I tan easily without having to stretch out for hours lathered in suntan oil.'

She glared at him resentfully, daring him to say one more word about her abusing her position.

'There's no need to drape that towel around yourself,' he said mildly, ignoring the expression on her face. 'I'd really never noticed before, but you have a nice body. Not too thin.'

There was gleaming amusement as his eyes met hers, and she could have hit him.

'Coming from an expert on women's bodies, I suppose I should be flattered,' she said tightly, 'but I'm not. Because I don't appreciate being sized up like a piece of meat.'

'Is that what I was doing?' he asked idly. 'I had no idea. You're obviously one of those women who finds it impossible to accept compliments.'

Her face was bright red now. She wished desperately that she could think of something cutting to say, but she couldn't.

'Is it because you feel insecure about the way you look?' he asked with interest, and she felt as though she were dying a million deaths.

'Spare me your attempts at psychology,' she muttered between her teeth.

'Do you?' he persisted.

She could feel her body trembling. She didn't even dare stand up and walk back to the hotel, because she wasn't entirely sure that her legs would support her.

Did he find all this amusing? Did he think that their familiarity of sorts entitled him to make sweeping, insulting generalisations about her?

'I'm perfectly happy with the way that I look,' she bit out. 'I may not look like a model, but there's more to life than appearances, anyway.'

Now I sound defensive, she thought miserably. She wished that he would just go away and leave her alone.

'You're right,' he agreed, releasing her from the stranglehold of his blue eyes and gazing around him with appreciation. 'That pool looks damned inviting.' He stood up and flexed his muscles. 'Mind if I get into some swimming-trunks and join you?'

Christina shielded her eyes and stared up at him. It's a public pool, she wanted to inform him; you can come back down here, but I'm sure as hell not going to be around.

'Please yourself,' she said, leaning over to pick up a magazine from the ground. She stretched out on her towel, not looking in his direction as he walked back towards the hotel.

The peaceful calm of the past few days seemed like a lifetime away. Now she would be tense every time he was around, watching him, over-aware of his every movement, reading all kinds of things into his remarks. You'd think that the mere fact of their having grown up in each other's houses would have made her more or less immune to his impact, but if anything it exaggerated it. She looked at the man and could also see the boy, and that made her response to him confusingly intense.

She walked back to her room very quickly, hoping that she wouldn't have the misfortune to bump into him on the way up, and she didn't.

Later, as she joined the others at the bar for drinks, she realised that much of that laid-back relaxation which they had enjoyed together had vanished.

Their numbers had increased twofold, what with the models—Frances and a raven-haired beauty called Janessa—and their entourage, and of course Adam.

He glanced at her briefly as she walked towards the group, and then returned to his conversation with one of the crew, a middle-aged man called Sam whom the group tended to regard as a father-figure.

Frances was standing next to him, not touching him, but making it obvious that they were an item. She looked sickeningly elegant in a clinging turquoise dress, designed only for those with supreme self-confidence about their appearance, and Christina suddenly felt horribly plain in her loose-fitting flowered culottes and matching shirt.

A sudden thought struck her: was Adam's unexpected appearance over here grounded in more prosaic reasons? Namely that Frances was here and relaxing with her, his lover, in the tropics for a few days was an irresistible attraction? Sure, he could throw in some valuable on-the-spot observations, but no doubt that was just an added bonus.

They had all decided to eat at the hotel and then participate in the party which was being given afterwards for the guests, but Adam informed them that they would have to count him out.

'Promised to visit a couple of old friends over here,' he said, and Christina didn't know whether she was relieved or disappointed.

It would certainly be less stressful without him around, but would it be as invigorating? This reaction irritated her and she composed her features into a polite smile of interest and insincere regret at his absence.

The others were trying to persuade him to stay and she firmly kept her mouth shut. That would be taking hypocrisy just a little too far.

Above the heads, his eyes met hers and he gave her a knowing, mocking little look which she met with bland indifference.

As he turned to leave, Frances slipped her arm through his and gazed up at him with a mixture of awe and adoration.

'We'll see you later,' she called out in a high, breathless voice which made Christina wince. Good grief, this was the beauty who also possessed brains? From where she was standing, she seemed the original bubble-head, bowled over by Adam's heady combination of power, good looks and charm.

What on earth would they talk about when they were alone together? She found that she was standing there, staring at nothing, her mind going round in frustrating circles, and she had to make a mental effort to pull herself together.

But the remainder of the evening was already lost on her. She made a good job of pretending that she was entering into the swing of things, dancing along with everyone else, but ever so often she would find her mind wandering off to Adam, like a stubborn dog determined to stray from its leash, and when that happened she would make an extra effort to concentrate on whoever was with her.

She also found that she was drinking far more than she normally did. The drinks were alluring, heady cocktails with rum and local fruit juices that only seemed to start having any effect when it was much too late to do anything about it.

It did have the distinct advantage of putting her in more of a party mood, however, and by midnight she found that she was really having a very good time indeed. So, it seemed, was the man with whom she was dancing, and who, from the expression on his face, found her quite amusing and witty.

She was giggling at something which, in her blurry state of mind, had seemed wildly funny, when she happened to glance up and right into Adam's eyes.

He was standing by the door with Frances leaning against him, his arm circling her waist, and he was looking directly at her.

Christina smiled broadly at him and waved, nearly teetering over in the process. Not, she thought blearily, that he seemed to appreciate her good humour. Not judging from the dark expression on his face as he forged a way through the crowds to where she was still dancing with the man, identity unknown.

He had disengaged Frances from him. Christina could just see her pouting in the company of Janessa, who had made remarkably little effort to socialise during the evening. No doubt the pair of them would find a certain sympathy moaning together. The thought made her grin even harder, though it evaporated when, a few seconds later, she felt her arm being held in a vice-like grip.

'The lady's with me,' Adam informed her dancing partner, who retreated, nodding.

'I'm not with you,' Christina pointed out, punctuating her observation with a little hiccup at the end. 'So there.'

Adam wasn't listening. He was too busy dragging her across the room towards the exit.

'What the hell are you playing at?' he demanded as soon as they were outside. 'You've drunk far too much. You're not accustomed to drink. It goes to your head. Now where the hell's your bedroom key?'

Christina wanted to protest. She also wanted to inform him that he was most definitely not the appointed guardian of her moral well-being, but her tongue appeared to be glued to the roof of her mouth.

She fished the key out of her tiny purse and he took it away from her, his face still grim.

'This is the last thing I expected to be doing with you,' he muttered, pulling her towards the lift. 'I would have thought that you would have more sense than to ply yourself with cocktails.'

'I'm terribly sensible,' Christina agreed, fumbling over her words, and she smiled up at him. She didn't feel terribly sensible at the moment. Her head was swimming and she knew, in that little part of her still rational, that in the morning she would probably wake up with a crashing hangover. Not a pleasant prospect.

He had reached her bedroom door. He unlocked it and escorted her inside, turning to switch on the light.

She had left the air-conditioner running and the room was beautifully cool. Wonderfully cool.

'I'm fine,' she told him, shaking her hair away from her face. 'I'm marvellous, in fact. On top of the world. I can take care of myself from here.'

'You couldn't tie your own shoelace,' he replied brusquely, then he began rummaging through her drawers.

'What are you doing?' Christina asked with interest.

He turned to face her briefly, his blue eyes impatient. 'What do you think? Or have you gone beyond the ability to think? I'm going to get you into bed.'

CHAPTER SEVEN

CHRISTINA felt a little groggy, true enough, but not so groggy that she didn't feel a very real quiver of alarm run through her.

'I don't need your help,' she managed to say, sitting on the edge of the bed. Her head was beginning to feel a little strange and she had a sudden, desperate desire to go to sleep.

'Now's not the time for your usual stubbornness.' He had found her pyjamas, blue and white striped shorts and a matching top with buttons down the front, and he eyed them sceptically.

'I don't like those awful things with lace and plunging necklines,' Christina said defensively, spoiling the impact of her remark with a wide yawn.

She lay back on the bed and closed her eyes. She was drifting on a cloud somewhere very calm and peaceful.

With a muttered oath, Adam began taking off her shoes, and she protested feebly that she wanted him to leave her room. Immediately. What would everyone think? What would Frances think?

'This isn't Paddington station,' he pointed out, pulling her up into a sitting position. 'There's no one around. As for Frances, she's an enjoyable part of my life...'

'But only for the moment?' Another wide yawn and a lazy stretch that felt good.

'Maybe,' he said softly, 'but maybe not. Maybe she's just the sort of woman I should marry—beautiful and not the sort to relish nights in in front of the fire and

120

days spent in front of a stove. She's definitely no clinging vine. What do you think?'

His words hurt; she could feel that even through the pleasant haze wrapped around her. There was a sting of unshed tears in her eyes, but it was too much effort to cry. Anyway, crying was the one thing she would never do in front of him.

'Is that why you're here?' she asked, voicing her suspicions of earlier on. 'To see whether she's marriage potential?'

'Would that be such a bad idea?'

'I don't know. I don't care. Why are you asking me all these questions when all I want to do is go to sleep?'

'Why indeed?' he murmured, but her eyes were closed and his voice was a muddled background sound.

He unzipped her dress at the back and she lay back down on the bed, heavily, looking at him from under her lashes. She knew that she shouldn't be here, in this dangerous situation, with her heart thudding a mile a minute, but her limbs were as heavy as lead.

Four cocktails, she thought dimly. Most normal people could gulp down twice that number and still be perfectly in control. But then, she acknowledged, most people were probably more used to drink than she was. She hardly ever touched the stuff and she certainly had no idea as to what her limits were.

He reached to tug down her dress and the contact of his hands on her shoulders made her skin burn.

His face, though, was expressionless, as if he was quite accustomed to doing this sort of thing. Which he probably was, she thought. Or at least the undressing part. She doubted he had much experience in the field of helping inebriated women into bed. Frances of the marriage potential didn't strike her as the sort to become inebriated. Hair out of place? Make-up every which way?

The thought made her giggle and their eyes met for an instant, then he lowered his and gently eased her dress off her.

Underneath the fine cotton, she was completely naked except for a pair of briefs. She could see the rise and fall of her breasts, the nipples hardened by the cool air pouring out of the air-conditioner.

She wondered what it would be like if he reached out and touched them. They were aching to be caressed. She had to fight hard to stifle the groan of desire that was spreading through her. She wasn't thinking straight, she knew that, but for some reason she still couldn't get her act together.

'Sit up,' he commanded shortly, averting his eyes from her nudity.

'You're emba...embarrassed,' she giggled again, a little hysterically this time, and she saw a dull flush creep into his face.

'Don't be ridiculous,' he said roughly, 'I've seen a naked woman before.'

She was breathing quickly, oddly uninhibited by her state of undress. She might not be a raving beauty, but she had never been ashamed of her body. As far as bodies went she was, in fact, rather proud of it: slim, long-legged, with a small waist and full breasts. She relaxed back on the bed, supporting herself on her elbows, and looked at him as he unbuttoned her pyjama top and held it out to her.

Was it her imagination or did he look decidedly less in control than he had when they had first entered the bedroom?

'Get your arms in here,' he said gruffly, sitting on the bed next to her, and she gave him a wide smile, then she stretched, a feline movement that stretched the muscles in her neck and made her feel much better.

'Don't do that,' he muttered, and she looked at him, wide-eyed.

'Why not?'

'Just get dressed, would you?'

She slipped her arm into one of the sleeves, then the other, and wondered dreamily how it was possible to feel so relaxed.

The world was spinning around, but gently.

He reached to button the top and she stopped him, moving his hand to cover the full swell of her breast.

Oh, God, this was sheer madness. She knew that even though the train of thought was a little blurry. But it was a madness she suddenly, desperately, wanted to explore. She arched back and with a stifled groan he rubbed his fingers over her swollen nipple. He was breathing quickly and unsteadily, and she felt as though she were in the grip of an overwhelming fever that was draining what little resources she had left.

He reached out with the other hand until he was caressing both her breasts, rolling his thumb on her nipples and sending darts of pleasure through her.

So this, then, was the nature of passion. She had never in her life experienced anything like it before.

She closed her eyes, tilting her head back, willing him to continue the marvellous exploration of her body. She could feel her body burning under his touch, then his mouth was playing on her breasts and she moaned with ecstasy as his tongue flicked the aching peaks.

She was hardly aware of reaching out, drawing his dark head harder against her. She could have gone on forever, but he abruptly pulled himself free and stood up.

Christina opened her eyes. Her body was still moist and trembling and she could see that he was as feverish as she was.

'Oh, God,' he muttered, running his fingers through his hair and looking away from her, 'I must have been crazy just then.'

His words were like a bucket of cold water over her, and had the instant effect of doing what no amount of black coffee could have done. They sobered her.

She looked down in confusion and began buttoning up her pyjama top, desperate now to cover herself. She didn't know what to say. Of course she could blame it on the drink, and the drink certainly had been responsible for lowering her inhibitions, but beyond that she had responded with a fervour that now frightened her.

She had wanted him, desperately, and she knew that if she was to be honest with herself that desire had nothing to do with four cocktails.

She still felt aroused even now, and that alone made her want to die.

'I had no intention of taking advantage of the situation,' he said under his breath, and Christina looked away. If that was what he thought, then she had no intention of persuading him otherwise. She knew that she had invited his response, but the last thing she wanted to do was to show him how much she had wanted him.

'It was my mistake as well,' she conceded grudgingly. She slipped on the striped shorts without looking at him at all.

Her head felt as clear as a bell, and all she wanted now was to be on her own.

'If you don't mind,' she continued, her eyes still averted, 'I'm all right now. Thank you for bringing me back to the room.' She almost choked on saying that, but she had every intention of retreating from this disastrous fiasco with as much of her dignity intact as possible.

He looked as if he might say something further and she found that she was holding her breath, willing him to leave. She didn't feel she could face him a moment longer. Those eyes saw too much and she didn't want them to see what she was feeling right now: humiliated, confused, vulnerable.

He turned around and walked out of the room, closing the door with a click behind him, and Christina felt her body sag, then she stood up and went across to the door and locked it.

The effect of the drink had vanished. Unfortunately. Because it meant that her thoughts were horribly lucid.

She switched off the light and lay down on the bed, staring up at the ceiling in the darkness.

How could she have been such a fool? Had her reaction to him been a throw-back to that burning, intense infatuation she had felt all those years ago, or worse, had she always been attracted to him, even when she'd thought that she had successfully recovered from her girlish lovesickness?

Not that it mattered. The fact remained that she had been consumed with passion. She closed her eyes, horrified at the image of herself, provocative and abandoned. She had never, ever done that with anyone in her life before, and if anyone had told her that she would behave like that in front of Adam Palmer she would have laughed in their face.

How was she going to live that awful episode down? She hoped that he would not gloat. Maybe he was gloating now, she thought. Deep down she knew that he was not the type, but she continued to torture herself. She imagined him letting himself into Frances's room, lying on the bed with her, telling her about his amusing little adventure. Frances, the woman he wanted to marry;

that she remembered with desperate, depressing clarity. Oh, God.

She imagined him snickering at the thought that still waters ran deep, that plain little Tina had practically begged for him to make love with her. The ugly duckling had tried to act the part of the seductive swan.

She held her hands over her face and tasted the salty tears as they trickled down her cheeks.

She must never let him know how badly the whole thing had affected her. She would pretend that it was a little, laughably unfortunate blip on an otherwise well ordered life should he mention a word. She would toss her head and joke that she would have to keep away from the demon drink.

She fell asleep and awoke the following morning with a crashing headache.

She dragged herself out of the bed, took two aspirin, and, for the first time since she had arrived, applied a generous helping of make-up to camouflage the pallor of her face and the dark shadows under her eyes.

She had no idea how she was going to face him, but she didn't have to, because when she arrived at the large, sunny room where breakfast was served it transpired that he had not yet come down.

Everyone else was there, though, including Frances, who gave her dark looks but didn't say a word, and they were all much too excited about the carnival to spare much thought for Christina.

They had decided to split into two groups to cover the maximum amount of ground. There were quite a number of bands, the costumes would all be fabulous, and it seemed a shame not to make full use of their resources.

Christina felt the stirrings of excitement that always accompanied a new job. And this one was going to be more challenging than most. She would have to photograph an atmosphere as much as anything else, and that called for a tremendous amount of skill.

She and Jennifer were going to go their own way, with Sam and the photographer whose job she was doing. They agreed to go as a foursome, but to branch out if the situation demanded it.

They all trooped out of the hotel with still no sign of Adam, and it was only when they were in the taxi, on their way downtown, that that haunted feeling left her.

Everywhere there were crowds of people, thousands of them. The streets echoed with music. Even when you couldn't actually hear any, you could feel it, as though it had worked its way to your bones and stayed there.

But it was the sight of the costumes that brought an awe-inspired silence to the group. They had dropped off at the meeting-point for one of the bigger bands, and now, standing in the square, Christina looked around her, dazzled by the display of colour and imagination. Everywhere there was a swirling of bright costumes. Groups of friends, attired in similar magnificent designs, talked together. She could hear the excited laughter in their voices and then she pulled out her camera and seemed to become one with the ambience. She completely forgot the presence of the other three. They were all adults, they could take care of themselves, but she simply had to drink in every single little sight around her.

She had brought several rolls of film with her, and she realised that she would have to be careful or else she would end up exhausting her supply on just one band, when there were others to see.

It was an unbelievable spectacle: hundreds and hundreds of people, all dressed in their blazing costumes, comprising a band, and each band carried its own theme, so that every different costume was fundamentally linked to the other.

And everything shimmered under the heat. The sound of the steel band began, the revellers grouped into their sections, and the dancing began.

Christina had no idea where the others had vanished to. She looked around her and then decided to abandon the attempt. She let herself be carried along by the music and by the sheer volume of people.

As the band crossed through the streets she branched away, leaving it behind to join another, winding its way along like an enormous, surrealistic snake, and all the time her fingers were clicking madly on her camera as she tried to capture everything.

She was hardly aware of the day flying past. She grabbed some lunch from a vendor at the side of the street and bought a cup of water which she desperately needed, and carried on.

By six in the evening, she realised that she was running on sheer momentum, and by the time she finally made it back to the hotel at a little after seven her feet were killing her.

Rather than return immediately to her room, she went to one of the bars for something long and cool to drink. Not very many people were around. They were still enjoying the tail-end of the day, she assumed, and gearing themselves up for the following day, when the spectacle would be repeated but in a grander style. The bands would be competing in front of judges, every costume would be meticulously in place, and Christina planned on taking at least an extra three rolls of film to be on the safe side.

She was sitting on a bar stool, sipping from a tall glass of ice-cold lime juice, when a familiar voice said from behind her, 'And how are you feeling today?' He signalled to one of the bartenders and ordered himself a drink.

Christina looked at him reluctantly. She had almost managed to put last night's disaster to the back of her mind. Now it re-emerged with unwelcome clarity.

'Fine, thank you,' she said a little stiffly.

He wasn't looking at her at all, though, and the contours of his face were rigidly polite. He wasn't, she realised, going to mention a thing about their little episode. He was treating her with the cool courteousness of a fairly distant acquaintance. Gone was that edge of familiarity that generally underlay their conversations, even when they were arguing.

'Good,' he said, 'and I take it you've had a field-day with your camera?'

She looked straight into his blue eyes and he looked back at her, blandly. After their previous clashes, this was just the kind of polite chit-chat she had longed for. Now, though, she found that it was oddly unsettling.

What a fool you are, she told herself. What do you want from Adam Palmer? His ridicule at your behaviour last night or his gentlemanly silence? Except it wasn't gentlemanly. It was more indifferent, and she discovered with alarm that his indifference was the last thing she wanted.

'Yes, I have,' she replied, in the same tone of voice. 'I've never seen anything quite so amazing—the colours, the sheer imagination out there.' She took another sip from her drink, quite pleased with the veneer of casualness which she was managing to get across, despite the fact that on the edge of her mind little flashing playbacks of the night before kept skimming past. 'But I suppose it's nothing new to you. You've been here before and seen it all.'

'Seen it all before? I don't think that's possible. It changes every year, and besides, it's been a long time since I was this way.' He took a long swallow of his drink and looked at her. 'What are your plans for tomorrow?'

'Much the same as today.' She shrugged. 'I want to go to the savannah so that I can see all of the bands as they line up for the judging. That way I won't miss anything. What about you? Were you out there today?'

He nodded. 'Frances and I managed to see quite a bit.'

Christina felt a painful knot in her stomach. She couldn't seriously be jealous, could she? That was just too laughable for words.

'Did she have a good time?' She thought of that long, blonde figure swaying to the music in the streets, and felt slightly sick.

'She knows how to enjoy herself,' Adam remarked, and Christina muttered under her breath,

'I'm sure she does.'

'She can be quite uninhibited when it suits her,' he continued in the same slightly speculative voice.

'Really?' This is all terribly uninteresting, her voice implied.

'But then,' he added slowly, 'so, I've discovered, can you.'

He looked at her with a certain hesitancy. 'I'm not sure how I'm going to phrase this,' he said at last, 'but the reason I just said that was really because of what happened last night.' He held up his hand as though he wanted to continue uninterrupted, but in fact the last thing she was going to do was interrupt. His words had taken her breath away. In fact they had taken her power of speech away completely.

There was a thundering noise in her head, beating on and on, as she sat there, stone-like, and listened in silence.

'You must be careful, Tina,' he said slowly. 'You're not accustomed to drink. I know that. Remember when you were fifteen and Fiona persuaded you to drink a bottle of red cordial which turned out to be laced with alcohol? You could hardly stand up afterwards and you felt lousy for three days.'

Christina remembered the episode well enough. Adam had been back from university, taking a few weeks off before he began that trip round Europe which was to end prematurely with the death of his parents. Thanks to Fiona, she had been obliged to spend three days at their house, thoroughly under the weather, and he had found the entire thing highly entertaining.

'What are you getting at?' she whispered. She knew what he was getting at, but some part of her wanted to hear him say it.

'I'm being honest with you, Tina,' he said, and she hated the tone of his voice when he said that. If he expected some kind of thanks for sitting there and insulting her, however well intentioned he thought he was being, then he was in for an unpleasant surprise.

'You could have had real problems if someone else had been in that room with you last night,' he continued slowly.

'Well, thank heavens that *you* were,' she said, stung because, without realising it, he was rubbing salt into an open wound. 'What a knight in shining armour you are. And thank you so much for pointing out my foolish behaviour to me.' She swallowed the remainder of her drink and stood up. 'I don't need you playing big brother with me, though,' she spat out. 'Save that for your sister.' She turned around and began walking away, and he

followed her, catching up with her and forcing her to
face him.

'I'm not trying to embarrass you,' he said tersely. 'I'm
just giving you a piece of friendly advice.'

'I don't want your friendly advice!'

She met his stare with hostility.

'You're so damned innocent!' he said harshly, and she
clenched her fists to her sides, tempted to lash out and
hit him, but knowing that that would serve no purpose
at all except to demean her still further.

'Are you quite finished?' she asked, in a dangerously
still voice. She felt as though her body was being held
under control through sheer force of effort, and that
any moment that effort would abandon her and she
would start trembling all over.

'You don't know the male species,' he ground on vehemently. 'You talk loud and hard about having been
taught a lesson by Robinson, but you're as naïve as they
come. I'm not saying that you make it a habit to encourage men when you've had a little too much to
drink...'

Oh, God, this was getting worse by the minute. She
thought back to her behaviour the night before and
wanted to cringe. She couldn't even deny that what he
was saying was true, because it was.

'I'm just telling you to be careful.' He shot her an odd
look. 'You've never slept with a man before, have you?
You never slept with Robinson, did you? Was that why
you two parted company?' he asked, and she stiffened
under his grip. 'I'm right, aren't I?' he said, reading the
expression on her face correctly. 'I guessed as much.' He
released her and she immediately pulled back.

'You can keep your guesswork to yourself,' she informed him tightly. 'You can keep it the same place you
keep your advice!'

She turned around without giving him an opportunity to reply and walked quickly towards the lift. She was half afraid that he might follow her into the lift and subject her to a few more of his charming observations on her personality and her sex life, but he stayed where he was, staring at her.

Once in her bedroom, she had a long shower, closing her eyes and letting the fine spray of water wash over her as if in some way it could cleanse that awful, exposed feeling that she had inside.

He had forced her to face a lot of things about herself and she hated it. What gave him the right to try and tell her how she should or should not behave? What gave him the right to make sweeping assumptions about her love-life? He had taken one look at her face and had known that she was a virgin. Was she so transparent? She was not ashamed of her virginity, but to have him confront her with it made her want to curl up with shame.

What would he make of that? she wondered bitterly. A far cry from the women he knew, she suspected. No doubt he found it yet another little amusing feature about her, like her dedication to her career and her avoidance of nightclubs.

She felt too exhausted to join the others for dinner, so she indulgently had some sent up to her room, and at a little after ten Jennifer, whom Christina now felt that she had known for years, came in for a chat and to discuss their plan of action the following day.

'You lost us,' she accused, sitting on the edge of the bed, and Christina made an effort to smile at the redhead.

'Not on purpose. I got a little carried away with the camera. Photographer's weakness.'

They spent the next half-hour enthusing over what they had seen that day, and then made arrangements for the following day: in the morning, photos of the models, unstaged shots of them posing amid the colourful chaos of the costumes, and after that they agreed to go their separate ways if they wanted.

Where, Christina wondered, would Adam be while all this was going on?

She should have known, of course. The following morning he was right there with them for the shoot of the models. Christina did her best to ignore him, but she seemed to have developed some extra sixth sense that picked up his presence wherever he happened to be.

When he came to stand next to her as she photographed Frances amid a group of band members who were costumed as magnificent butterflies, with huge wings shimmering in the breeze, she could feel her body tense, and then go into overdrive, bringing her out in a fine perspiration.

Sooner or later she would have to talk to him, she knew that, but after what had been said between them the evening before she couldn't bring herself to act normally. So she ignored him and concentrated on her camera, giving directions to Frances, and liaising with the other members of the crew.

'This is the first time I've seen you in action,' Adam said, his hands in his pockets. 'You're good.'

'It's my job,' Christina replied bluntly. 'I wouldn't have very much work if I didn't do it properly. There's a lot of competition out there and I have to keep on top of it.'

She moved off, leaving him where he was. So what if he was the boss? That didn't mean that she was obliged to humour his passing interest in what she was doing.

She looked at Frances through the camera lens. The colours of the dancing butterfly wings rebounded off her, giving her a rich, high colour, and her straight blonde hair was wild and tousled. She projected just the right unkempt, seductive image that matched well with the abandon that the carnival represented.

Christina had a good feeling about these photos. They would be superb. It would not be one of those instances when the camera reproduced a disappointing shadow of what was really viewed at the time.

She wound up as the steel band began to play, preluding the start of the winding march through the streets towards the savannah.

She carefully packed away her camera and looked around. Adam was staring at Frances, his face quite expressionless. Christina followed the direction of his gaze to Frances, her lovely face raised to the sun, brushing a strand of golden hair away from her face. The light captured her in a posture of pagan enjoyment, and Christina felt a little stab of glass pierce through her heart.

Perhaps, if she looked at herself honestly, she would have to admit that she rather envied that sheer power to attract, on a purely physical level, that Frances possessed.

If she had had that quality, would Adam have been able to resist her behaviour in the hotel room? Would he have walked away and later casually offered her advice on how to conduct herself?

Frances slowly turned to face Adam. She was quite aware of her own startling beauty and that knowledge was written on her face.

They suit each other, Christina thought acidly, packing up her equipment and looking away, both physically eye-catching, a photographer's dream with their startling contrast of fair and dark.

'Beautiful, isn't she?'

Christina hadn't heard him approach, but now Adam was standing right next to her, and the suddenness of his presence made her heart skip a beat. She glanced up briefly and then looked away, continuing what she had been doing.

'I saw you looking at her,' he carried on lazily. 'I expect those shots of her will be quite spectacular.'

'I expect so,' Christina said non-committally. 'She has good bones, the sort of face that the camera loves.' She looked past him to where Frances was moving away with some of her entourage. 'I think she's escaping,' she said lightly. 'You'd better run and catch up with her, because she'll be swallowed up in these crowds in no time at all.'

'So she will,' Adam commented with a little shrug. 'She's a big girl now, though. She hardly needs my protection.'

Christina didn't answer. She began to move away and he fell into step beside her.

'I'm a big girl too,' she said edgily, 'and I don't need your protection either.'

'I'm sure you don't,' Adam replied smoothly. 'If anything untoward happens to you, I promise I won't interfere. But I will come along with you, see what sort of scenes you intend to capture. That way, if Bill needs my advice on any aspect of writing this article I'll be more capable of providing it.'

Much as she would have liked to argue with that one, she couldn't. Apart from anything else, he had a valid right to accompany her, see her in action, any time he pleased. He would, after all, be handing over a very generous cheque for her efforts over here.

Anyway, they had known each other for years. He would be surprised if she objected strongly to his company. He might even guess the reason behind it— that he made her nervous, that she was too aware of him for her own good.

'Of course,' she said tartly. 'Follow me by all means. Although I doubt I'll be as exciting company as your girlfriend.'

With that she moved off, thinking, Make what you like of that, I don't care.

CHAPTER EIGHT

THIS was the final day of the carnival. Yesterday, the Monday, there had been an air of disorganised festivity. Today, though, it was different. The bands seemed somehow more complete. The different sections were rigidly defined, whereas the day before people had crossed over from one section to another, so that the costumes had become intermingled.

Of course, there was a reason for this. The bands were to be judged today.

Christina found herself chatting to Adam about the differences in the atmosphere on the Monday and the Tuesday, and he, in turn, chatted to her about the origins of carnival in general. He was well informed.

They walked along the pavements, frequently being separated by people barging past them, linking back up, amicably chatting about everything that was going on around them. And Adam, she had to admit, could be an amusing companion. It hardly surprised her. She had always known him to be witty, with that dry incisiveness that came naturally to some people.

After the initial tension of realising that he would be spending the day in her company, she had found herself beginning to relax. And the fact that she had to devote a good proportion of her time to her professional duties made things a whole lot easier.

By lunchtime, she was unwillingly enjoying herself. They ate *roti*, bought from a vendor at the side of the road—parcels of curried beef and chicken which they held in their hands. The curried sauce dripped down the side of their faces, but it was delicious—hot and spicy and surprisingly welcome, more so than a salad, which Christina would have imagined to be far nicer in weather such as this.

They bought soft drinks, ice-cold, sold at exorbitantly over-inflated prices, and drank straight from the can.

Crowds of people swarmed around them, even though they had left the main road and found a side-street in which to relax for a while.

All the time there was a dazzling array of potential photographs: people sitting on the pavements, legs stretched out, expressions of sheer exhaustion on their faces; little children being carried on the shoulders of their fathers, bouncing up and down to the sounds of the deafening music; the amazing colours and designs of the costumes, swaying this way and that as their wearers danced along to the beat of the music. Ever so often, so many images would present themselves that Christina was literally spoilt for choice.

They had finished lunch and were rejoining one of the bands, from the sidelines, when Adam murmured into her ear, 'You really enjoy what you do, don't you? Every nerve in your body seems to be alive.'

'This is quite spectacular,' Christina admitted, turning to him and seeing something in his eyes which she couldn't identify, but which made her feel momentarily unsteady. 'Of course, I love what I do, but this——' she gesticulated around her '—this is magnificent. I hardly need to focus the camera at all. I get the feeling that, if I just hold it up and point the lens in any direction, whatever emerges will be inspired.' Her eyes were bright. She felt as though the reckless abandon all around her was somehow contagious, and she had been infected with it.

They were being half pushed along by the crowds, caught up in their peculiar, rhythmic shuffle which harmonised perfectly to the music.

Adam slipped his arm loosely around her shoulder, and she found herself linking her fingers through his. Wariness, caution, that instinct to draw up her defences every time she was with him, seemed inappropriate in this wild atmosphere.

She grinned up at him and he bent down to brush her lips lightly with his.

Christina pulled back with a jerk and his fingers tightened over hers so that she could not pull out of his hold. Not that she really wanted to. She liked the heavy feel of his arm around her, the closeness of his body, as filmed with perspiration as her own was.

Everyone seemed to have their arms around someone else. There was a lot of innocent, joyous physical contact, and just for a while it was easy, all too easy, to forget her inhibitions, to imagine that she was the sort of stunning companion that he favoured, to forget the shortcomings of which she had been made all too painfully aware by Greg. She even found herself forgetting all about Frances, even though her image hovered on the outskirts of her consciousness, the little nagging voice of common sense to which she had temporarily closed her ears. Common sense was too mundane for this sort of explosive atmosphere, which was going to her head like a steady stream of alcohol.

She relaxed and her body moulded softly against the hard contours of his own.

They made their way to the savannah. Adam had somehow managed to get them special permits that allowed them access to photograph the bands passing on to the stage from a privileged position, and he released her to drink from a can of ice-cold pop, while she snapped a series of pictures with professional ease. In between shots, he reached out to hand her the can, and she drank from it, savouring the long gulps of ice-cold liquid.

When he came to stand next to her, and began asking her questions about what she was shooting, she answered breathlessly, her colour alive with the excitement of the occasion.

'Wait a minute,' he said, and before she could object he took the camera away from her and was taking pictures of her, her face half laughing, half surprised, her hair everywhere.

'You never told me you were a photographer!' she laughed as he handed the camera back to her, and he said with a wry grin,

'I'm not. So don't expect masterpieces when you develop that roll of film. When I was a boy, I had a knack of taking those clever shots that somehow manage to chop heads and limbs off of people, and I've only improved slightly since then.'

Christina laughed, throwing her head back. Everything was conspiring to make her feel bold and sensuous, and the expression in those blue eyes staring back at her seemed to be telling her something. What, she couldn't put her finger on, but something that seemed ridiculously alluring in this heat.

She turned away and continued snapping, eating her way through her rolls of film.

As the bands filtered one by one on to the raised stage, which was overlooked by rows upon rows of makeshift stands, filled to bursting with thousands of spectators, including the team of judges, the band members, costumed and full of energy, danced in an orgy of wonderful abandon.

Christina snapped women with their heads thrown back, their eyes closed, lost in the music and the ambience.

Where was Frances in all of this? Not very happy, wherever she was, that was for sure. She had made a point of displaying her possessiveness with Adam to everyone in the crew and she wouldn't be impressed at having found herself without him by her side.

The thought of the other woman was a dampener on her high spirits and Christina immediately shoved the image to the back of her mind.

She lay down her camera for a moment and stood with her hands on her hips, her head tilted back, staring at the ongoing spectacle taking place only a matter of yards away from her.

She felt Adam move towards her from behind, then his hands were on her shoulders, massaging them. Christina opened her mouth to protest, but instead of speaking she lapsed into silence, breathing deeply with enjoyment as his fingers kneaded the firm flesh of her back.

She half closed her eyes.

'Does that feel good?' he asked her, and she could hear the smile in his voice. Too good, she wanted to tell him, but how could she say that without betraying her feelings? As far as he was concerned, this was a friendly gesture, and no doubt he was swept up in the heat of the moment, anyway, just as she was. It might feel erotically pleasurable to her, but it would not feel that way to him.

The realisation made her body tense, and he murmured persuasively, 'Relax. Concentrate on the bands. Forget what I'm doing to you.'

Forget what he was doing to her? She wanted to laugh outright at that one, but she couldn't. Her mouth felt too dry and she was slowly beginning to realise why.

She was more than simply attracted to Adam Palmer. Mere physical attraction would have been inconvenient and embarrassing, but it would not have made her feel so giddy and alive whenever he was around.

No, that headiness had its roots in quite another origin. She was in love with him, hopelessly, passionately in love with him, even though, she now realised, it was something she had been desperately trying to hide from herself ever since they had found themselves thrown together in that cottage in Scotland.

The potent attraction which had hit her from the very moment she had become aware of him as a member of the opposite sex had subsided, lain in waiting, and now it was no longer just the sharp innocent tug of teenage attraction that she had once felt, but the deep, aching essence of love.

What she had felt for him as a girl had been hopeless infatuation. What she felt now was just as hopeless, but in a different league altogether. It was an adult's fierce passion, born from respect and admiration and cemented in desire.

The impact of her realisation snaked through her, making her shiver convulsively in the heat. How could this have happened? It was illogical, absurd. Years ago he had tactlessly handed her girlhood crush back to her. Had she forgotten that? Had she idiotically let herself think that a few years would have made him more receptive?

She was a plain Jane. Greg had told her so in no uncertain terms, and at the time, when she had recovered from the hurt of that insult, she had persuaded herself that he had done her a favour, that he had instilled a necessary caution in her dealings with the opposite sex.

So how could she have fallen in love with a man who didn't even breathe the same air as she did? They had known each other for years, but in this they might well have been two strangers from different planets. Adam Palmer was the man every woman wanted, and the man who refused to commit himself to any. Experience had taught him his own bitter lessons.

And she . . . she was the woman who scarcely rated a second glance, who had believed fervently that after Greg she would never allow herself to feel anything towards a man but friendship and a certain amount of contented attraction—certainly nothing like the agonising, confusing range of emotions stilling her powers of reasoning.

No wonder she had conveniently chosen to forget all about Frances's presence. Why, she thought with a stab of bitterness, let reality intrude when she could spend a few stolen hours pretending that it didn't exist?

She felt sick and dizzy and if she could have she would have fled, but she couldn't. She had no option but to keep this silly grin plastered across her face, like a circus clown, and pretend that everything was fine.

His fingers had moved down her back, working their way along her spine, and she eased herself out of his grasp.

She didn't think that she could face him; she would betray too much to those clever eyes of his.

So she wriggled her shoulders and said without looking around, keeping her voice light and even with a huge effort of will, 'That was just what the doctor ordered. You should take it up professionally.'

·'I'll bear that in mind should my businesses ever decide to go under,' he said drily from behind her.

His voice sent little threads of awareness shooting through her and she stooped to retrieve her camera and then moved away, closer to the stage, where one band was moving off and another was eagerly waiting to take its place.

'What's the matter?' Adam asked sharply, turning her around to face him, his long fingers coiled into her hair.

'Nothing,' Christina lied quickly. She knew that she was blushing, and she hoped that he would believe the heat was the reason behind it.

He gave her a disbelieving look. 'Really. One minute you were totally relaxed and carefree. Now, you're acting as though you've suddenly found something unpleasant in the soup. So out with it. What's wrong?'

'Honestly,' she persisted stubbornly, 'nothing.' She knew Adam, though. He was persistent. So she said with as much conviction as she could muster, 'Actually, I do have a bit of a headache. I guess it must be all the concentrating, combined with the noise and the heat.' She rubbed her temples meaningfully and shifted her eyes away from his powerful body to a clump of shrubbery slightly behind him.

Adam nodded. 'Is it very bad? Perhaps we ought to think about getting you back to the hotel. There's nothing worse than having a headache and knowing that it's going to get worse and worse. I've suffered from them occasionally and I know that it's not a pleasant experience.'

Christina wished he wouldn't show this amount of sympathy. A bit would have been fine, but there was something too understanding in his eyes as he looked down at her, and that made her feel guilty and uncomfortable.

'I'll be fine,' she muttered, backing slightly. She gave him a bright smile and he frowned.

'Are you sure that a headache is the only thing bothering you?' he pressed, and she laughed.

'What else? Besides, I can't go back to the hotel just yet. I have one last band to cover.'

'I'm sure you've already covered it. You were out here yesterday, don't forget. And we did manage to see most of the bands throughout the course of today. I can't have you collapsing on me in a heap because you think you're under pressure to stay out here in this blazing heat taking pictures until the cows come home.'

He moved towards her and she felt a surge of panic rise to her throat. She didn't want him close to her. That made her thoughts go into mad disarray, and what it did to her body didn't bear thinking about.

'I'll take a few more and then I'll return to the hotel,' she compromised insistently, desperately, and he nodded.

'A few,' he said in a warning voice, 'and that's it. Don't forget who's the boss here.' His voice was light, but there was a serious glint in his eyes as he surveyed her.

Christina turned away and refocused her attention on what was happening on the stage, but all of that carefree enthusiasm had evaporated. She was too conscious of him standing right there beside her, dark and threatening, a danger to her peace of mind.

All this brotherly sympathy irritated her. She didn't want it. She knew what she wanted; it was the sort of hungry response which she imagined a woman like Frances could arouse in him. She wanted him to look at her and feel the same fierce, uncontrollable desire to reach out and touch as she felt for him.

She thought of herself, her mousy plainness, camouflaged just now under the warm glow of a tan, but as soon as that had faded she would revert to her old unremarkable self. It was laughable. She was laughable.

She concentrated on taking pictures, trying to ignore his presence, even though her body tingled with an awful awareness of him, when she felt his hand on her shoulder and he said into her ear, 'Enough. It's not getting any cooler. You'll probably faint in a minute if you're not careful.'

'If I do, I won't hold you responsible!' Christina snapped.

'I said put the camera down. We're going back to the hotel.' His voice was flat. He had decided and he was in no mood for a lively debate on the subject.

She shrugged and fiddled around with her equipment, not looking at him, wishing that he would vanish into a puff of smoke and leave her to get on with her life the way she had been doing before he stepped on to the scene.

They began walking away from the savannah, weaving in between the crowds of people.

The hotel was within walking distance of where they were, and as they cleared their way out of the savannah she could feel her feet beginning to ache. Wasn't that always the way? Sheer momentum could keep you going for hours, days, but the minute you relaxed all the aches and pains jumped on you and began pounding away.

They walked slowly and in silence. The streets were littered with debris: used paper cups, streamers from some of the costumes, actual headgear which had been discarded because of the weight at some point during the march to the savannah.

The blinding sun had dipped and twilight was beginning to set in. The descent from daytime into night was swift in the tropics. Within an hour it would be much darker. Christina glanced across at the figure striding alongside her, his hands in his pockets, the angles of his face unyielding. She had seen the boy grow into the youth, then into the man, and still she could feel an illicit thrill of awareness whenever she set eyes on him, as though he were a stranger with all the power in the world to disturb her. And wasn't he?

The streets were much emptier here than they had been further back. The onlookers would all have followed the bands to the savannah. They would move on to private parties as night fell. By midnight all that would be left of these two days of carnival would be the rubbish-strewn streets.

'My head feels a lot better,' Christina said, to break the silence.

'Good.' He spared her a brief glance and she wondered what was going through his mind.

'I suppose you're eager to get back to Frances,' she said, making herself remember the madness of what she felt, and he turned to her, his eyebrows raised.

'If I didn't know better, I'd say that you were jealous of her,' he said blandly. 'Are you?'

'Don't be absurd.' Christina laughed as heartily as she could. 'I'd be a wreck if I became jealous of every model I ever photographed. Or, for that matter, every wealthy person whose house I was ever invited into to take pictures of their pet budgies or rock gardens. I'm just not the jealous type.' Was she overdoing the spiel? she wondered. The fact was that she was ripped apart at the thought of Adam and Frances together.

'I would never have become so close to Fiona if I were the jealous type,' she continued, making sure that she rammed her point home, because to have him think that she was jealous of Frances was only a step away from having him think that she was jealous of the other woman because of her relationship with him. 'If you recall, my parents weren't from the same exalted background as yours. If they hadn't saved to put me through private school, I would never have come into contact with Fiona, would I? Our social circles would have been a thousand miles apart.'

'Did that bother you?' There was an element of curiosity and interest in his voice. This was what was so dangerous about him, she thought. When she wasn't angry with him, it was too disturbingly easy to be charmed by that talent he had for making her feel special. It didn't matter if intelligence and common sense told her that it was a talent which he used with every woman he ever spoke to.

'No, it didn't,' she said shortly. 'I had a very happy childhood. Why should I have been jealous?'

'Because that's the way human nature operates. Envy isn't a noble emotion, but, then again, how many of us are noble?'

'Are you envious of anyone?' Christina asked, turning the question round to him.

'Not that I can think of offhand.'

'Lucky you,' she said more sarcastically than she had intended. 'One of the noble few.'

'Merely philosophical,' Adam returned smoothly. 'Why waste time and effort on envy? That's how life passes you by. As far as I'm concerned you've got to get out there and achieve your maximum potential.'

You've certainly succeeded there, she wanted to inform him. Most men would kill for what Adam Palmer possessed—money, status, power, looks, brains. And, of course, his pick of women. In fact, she thought, most men would kill simply for the pick of women bit.

They had left the crowds way behind them. They turned off the savannah and began walking slowly up the incline that led to the hotel.

Dusk had settled over them, a shadowy darkness filled with the growing sounds of crickets chirping, insects calling to each other, frogs croaking in the bushes at the side of the road.

'So,' he spoke into the silence, 'you're not the jealous type. You don't smoke or keep late nights. You don't sleep around. So what vices have you got, little Tina Reynolds?'

Christina gritted her teeth. She didn't care for that description of her. Little Tina Reynolds? He made her sound like someone who had just progressed out of dolls and easy-to-read books. God knew what he would think if he knew beyond doubt that she had never slept with Greg, that when it came to the crunch the thought had frightened her and turned her off.

He also managed to make it sound as though vices were enormously exciting attributes, while she, devoid of any, was as dull as dish-water—weird and boring.

'I don't like men who patronise,' she answered calmly, choking down her anger.

'Meaning me?' He laughed softly under his breath as though he found her reaction amusing.

'If that's how you think of yourself, then yes,' she said, noticing that her reply didn't meet with quite the same level of amused mockery.

'And what do you think of me?' he asked casually, in a voice that implied that he was just passing the time of day. Or night. They happened to be walking together, his tone said, on a balmy night; this question was just for the sake of providing conversation.

She was quite certain that her answer didn't interest him in the slightest. But now that he had asked, why not tell him?

'I think,' she said carefully, 'that you're extremely intelligent and extremely well off, and you know it. You're well aware of the advantages both those things can bring, and you exploit those advantages to the full. Look at all the Frances look-alikes that waltz through your life, for instance.'

'There you go,' Adam drawled, 'harping on about Frances yet again...'

'I was not harping on. I was using her to cite an example.'

He ignored her interruption. 'What makes you think that the women I go out with are attracted to me because of my intelligence? Or my money for that matter?'

'Because...' Christina said, floundering '...because...'

'Because those are the qualities that attract you in a man? Greg didn't have a great deal of money and from all accounts he was hardly intelligent, except in that street-wise way that con men have, so what turned you on about him?'

She had the funny feeling that she had managed, somehow, to throw away her chance of giving him a few insights into his character. He had turned the tables on her so expertly that she was left trying to find an answer for his question, something glib and amused that would cover her confused outrage at his speculations.

We're not talking about me, she wanted to inform him in a light, cool voice; we're talking about you.

He was waiting for an answer. She could feel it in those vivid blue eyes fixed on her.

'Greg is none of your business,' she said stiffly, 'and, for your information, I don't give a damn about how much a man earns.'

They had reached the top of the incline. To the left the road branched off into a long drive that led up to the hotel. And, clustered to one side of the road, a scattering of trees and shrubbery threw shadows across the tarmac.

In the space of time it had taken them to make their walk back the greyness of the twilight had given way to the impenetrable blackness of night. There was no full moon, and next to her his body, turned towards her, was a dark outline, illuminated eerily by the intermittent overhead lamps.

'You're just attracted to their intelligence?' he asked. 'What *did* attract you to Greg? I'm curious. Some women like men who are wolves in sheep's clothing. Are you one of them?'

He had stopped walking and she reluctantly followed suit. She would have preferred to keep going, to get back to the hotel as quickly as she could, because being close to him was making her head pound. She felt as though she had just run a marathon. She was perspiring and her heart was thumping painfully.

'Why do you keep asking me about Greg?' she said coolly. 'Anyone would think that you were jealous of him.' That was spoken on the spur of the moment, and she didn't think that he would react to it, but he did. His face tightened and he glanced away before fixing his eyes on her.

'And why on earth would I be jealous of him?' he asked, but there was something just a shade too controlled about his voice. 'Do you think that it's always been some secret yearning of mine to waste my time trying to make an easy living by climbing on to the backs of other people? Or maybe you think I'm jealous because he tried to get you into bed?'

That caught her by surprise and she had to stop herself from gasping out loud. Of course, he was laughing at her, but his remark still unhinged her.

'This conversation is getting ridiculous,' she muttered, turning away, but he reached out to grip her arm, forcing her to remain where she was.

'What's the hurry? You still haven't answered my question.'

'It doesn't deserve an answer,' she informed him in a voice that was treacherously breathless. 'Anyway, there's nothing wrong with being attracted to a man for his intelligence, to get back to your original question.'

'And what about physical appeal?'

'What about it?' There was silence, and she continued defensively, 'I'm hardly one of life's great beauties. I know that. The last thing I would ever do now is involve myself with a man who was incredible-looking. Only beautiful women can hold men like that.'

'You don't really believe that, do you?'

The question irritated her. Couldn't he have been a gentleman and told her that of course she was attractive? Irrationally, it was what she wanted to hear, even though she knew that it would not have been the truth.

'Of course I believe it. They say that you attract to the level of your own attractiveness.'

'You have a distorted image of yourself.'

How odd, she suddenly thought, this intense conversation conducted between two weary individuals in the unlikely area of a hotel drive, with the dark shrubbery nestling around them. Odd and somehow dangerous, although she couldn't quite put her finger on the reason for that feeling. She had nothing to fear from him.

'I have a realistic image of myself,' she corrected, trying to control the wild, hot thudding in her veins. 'Don't get me wrong, I'm not unhappy with myself over something as trivial as appearance, but I'm not stupid. I wouldn't pretend to myself—or to anyone else, for that matter—that I'm the sort who makes heads swing round in the street.'

'Not many people are,' Adam said in a strange voice. 'There's an enormous difference between drop-dead beauty and attractiveness.'

'How generous of you to point that out,' Christina said, turning away and heading off towards the hotel, relieved that he was no longer holding her.

She shouldn't be out here, having this kind of conversation with a man who meant everything to her and to whom she meant nothing in return. She wasn't being fair on herself. In this life you had to look after your interests to the best of your ability, and a moron could have seen that this depth of personal intercourse was not very healthy for her interests.

She sensed rather than heard him coming up behind her, then she felt his hand on her arm, turning her around.

'What the hell do you think you're doing?' she gasped, trying to disentangle herself and failing.

'I'm proposing we continue this conversation. Right here.'

'I don't want to.'

'Well, I do.'

So that was it, was it? He wanted to indulge his curiosity about her, and he naturally expected her to oblige without demur. No doubt he also assumed that she should be flattered by his interest.

'And you always get what you want, is that it, Adam?' Her voice sounded uneven and breathless and that infuriated her because she wanted to be in control, even though her heart was beating like mad.

'Not always.' But 'almost always' was the unspoken implication. 'You were once attracted to me, albeit many years ago. Do you still find me physically attractive? Am I one of those off-putting men who you consider can only be held by a beautiful face?'

'You're good-looking, yes,' she said, ignoring the first part of his question. 'But you know that. I'm just stating the obvious, but, if you want to indulge your ego, then by all means do so. Now can you let me go? I'm tired, my feet are killing me and,' she finished on a burst of pure inspiration, 'my headache's coming back.'

'How convenient,' he replied, ignoring her request to be released.

The funny thing was that she really didn't feel all that well. His hand on her flesh was warm, sending little electric currents into her skin, and the intensity of those blue eyes, glittering black in the shadows, was making her feel weak and unsteady.

How could she have fallen in love with this man? Rather, why couldn't she have dismissed him from her mind, and her heart, all those years ago instead of carrying around his image like the refrain from a song that refused to go away?

He was looking at her as though quite prepared to carry on their conversation until the cows came home, and suddenly she felt utterly tired and very angry.

'It's not convenient,' she spat out, 'it's the truth! Why don't you go and pester someone else?' Frances, for instance, she wanted to shout. He would be welcome there.

'Don't talk to me like that!' he snapped back. His fingers bit into her flesh. She could feel her arm going slightly numb.

She gave a loud, incredulous laugh. 'Don't talk to you like that? And just who do you think you are to tell me how I should and shouldn't talk to you? You might be paying for my little sojourn over here, but I'm working for the privilege.'

He didn't answer. Instead, he began walking towards the hotel, with her in tow.

'Let go of me!' she repeated, struggling.

'I'm not finished with you.'

'I don't give a damn!'

'I do.'

He pulled her through the tiny arcade of shops, now all closed for the evening, towards the swimming-pool, which was deserted.

'Why now?' Christina asked as he installed her firmly on to one of the deckchairs and sat alongside her, preventing any escape. 'Why, after all these years, the sudden interest in the workings of my mind?' Her voice was laced with sarcasm.

'Why not? I always knew that you were interesting and I've recently rediscovered the fact.'

He always knew that I was interesting? What a joke.

'So now you're going to shove it down my throat until I choke? Has it occurred to you that the feeling might not be mutual? That I might not find you interesting in the slightest?'

'No.'

He reached out and trailed a finger along her cheek and Christina started back in shock.

'What are you doing?'

'I'm touching you,' Adam said, as though that explained everything. Her body froze as his touch continued its path along her collarbone, sending little shivery waves through her body. Under her T-shirt, she could feel her breasts aching, and as his finger found one pert nipple, circling it tantalisingly, she heard herself groan.

He was using all his expertise, all his knowledge of women, to seduce her. She could feel it, even though his touch was so light as to be almost feathery.

His knowledge of women, she thought dazedly. How many of them had there been, in and out of his life? He probably couldn't even remember their names. For God's sake, there was one very much in evidence in the same hotel as she was! Had she forgotten that little detail?

He had played with them, just as he was playing with her, except in this deadly game she would be the one to emerge wounded and distressed. She was in love with him, vulnerable to all that seductive charm. Love could make you do crazy things, but not this crazy.

She sat up abruptly and stepped over the side of the chair, her movement catching him unawares.

'Where are you going?' he asked point-blank.

'To my bedroom.' Then, before he could construe anything from that, she added with barely concealed hostility, 'Alone. I don't want you, Adam. You may have suddenly discovered my interest-quotient, but if you think that your passing curiosity about me is going to get me into bed with you then you're wrong. You can go to hell!' She spun around and began walking away. Quickly. The thought that he might follow her gave her feet wings, but when she paused by the side of the hotel to look round he was still sitting there.

Not even worth the chase, she thought with a mixture of relief and bitterness. He'll take his frustrations to Frances's bedroom, no doubt, and in the morning this little episode will be just a memory for him.

But what, she thought agonisingly, about me?

CHAPTER NINE

CHRISTINA had rehearsed her coolness, spent hours making sure that her mask of polite expressionlessness was firmly in place, only to discover that she might just as well not have bothered, because she didn't lay eyes on him for the next three days.

They were busy shooting the final pictures of the models, exploring beaches which would make attractive backdrops. There was an atmosphere of calm now that the carnival was over, and everyone was returning to their normal lives. The streets had slowly been cleared of debris. Bit by bit, all evidence of the bacchanalian festivities was being dismantled and swept away.

Where was Adam? Wherever he was, it wasn't with Frances, who was very much in evidence, preening and posing, making love to the camera, her body sensuous and feline. She had made sure that she stayed well out of the sun and her porcelain complexion was striking against the various shades of brown of everyone around her.

Christina had been rather proud of her golden colour, but now, as she stood under some palm trees on a wide white expanse of beach, deserted apart from their team and a few stray locals, she looked at Frances and wondered whether she hadn't overdone it on the tanning front. Had she become leathery?

She caught Frances's eye and was startled by the venom she saw. She had spent the past few days studiously keeping out of the other woman's way. Now she was about to do the same, trailing slightly behind everyone as she fiddled with her equipment, when Frances stopped ahead, waiting.

Christina eyed her resignedly.

'I've been meaning to have a word with you,' Frances said, tossing her blonde hair impatiently away from her face.

'Perhaps a bit later,' Christina suggested helpfully, feeling hot and jaded. 'They'll be waiting up ahead for us.'

It was late afternoon and the heat was beginning to fade slightly, but not enough to be anything like refreshing. She had been up since dawn and shooting since mid-morning. She just wanted to get back to the hotel and count the hours until the plane left and this nightmare job was at an end. She certainly wasn't in any kind of mood for a confrontation, and confrontation it would be. It was stamped all over Frances's perfectly formed face.

'Let them wait. This won't take long anyway. I just want to know what the hell is going on between you and Adam.'

'I have no idea what you're talking about,' Christina said, but her cheeks had turned pink with guilt.

'No? Then why are you blushing? If you could only see yourself! Do you seriously think that he would give you a second glance? You're nothing!' The finely chiselled features were rigid with anger. 'He has me!' she said on a high, barely controlled note. 'You're nothing next to me!'

What reply was there to that? It wasn't a biased observation; it was a statement of fact.

'He doesn't want you,' she hissed, looking at the rest of the crew quickly, over her shoulder, 'so don't start getting any ideas into that head of yours. You might be old chums or whatever, but stay out of his bed!'

'Or else what?' Christina felt compelled to ask, and two bright patches of colour appeared on Frances's cheeks.

'You won't hook him,' she said, her eyes as hard as diamonds. 'I'll make sure of that.'

She turned away and waved at the crew, who were beginning to look impatient. There was a smile on her face, one of the first that had not been directed towards the camera. No one would have guessed at the content of their conversation, but Christina felt as though she had been bombarded by a steamroller.

She could have kicked herself for having just stood there, gaping like a goldfish, but at the time her sheer astonishment at Frances's outburst had thrown her into silence.

Now, more than ever, she couldn't leave the island soon enough. She had been stupid and short-sighted and insane to have fallen in love with Adam, and she had no intention of compounding the horror of her situation by waging a silent war with his girlfriend.

She was about to slink off to her bedroom, once back at the hotel, when Sam, Adam's right-hand man on the shoot, signalled to her from the bar to join him for a drink. Frances had headed off to her bedroom, or Adam's bedroom, and Christina absent-mindedly sat on one of the bar stools, her mind whirring away at the thought of Frances and Adam together. She hardly took in Sam's initial comment, and when she did she did a double take.

Adam was ill. No passing cold or unwelcome hangover, but really ill. Ill, she was informed, as in bed-ridden for the past two days.

The idea of it shocked her, for some reason. She could not imagine him being ill; he was as strong as a horse,

immune to those ailments that afflicted mere mortals.
Wasn't he?

Sam was talking in a low, worried voice and most of
what he was saying was going over her head—fever,
severe stomach cramps, paralytic weariness. She listened
to the monologue, her head swimming.

'What has the doctor said?' she asked when there was
a break, and Sam shook his head.

'Some kind of fever, transmitted by mosquitoes ap-
parently.' His next words were like a body-blow. 'He
can't travel. He's got to stay here. He's going to be
transferred to his friend's house in Maraval some time
tomorrow, but Clive isn't going to be around after
tonight. He'll need someone to look after him.' He
looked at her levelly. 'You.'

Of course, she thought, as she headed towards his
bedroom five minutes later, it was out of the question.
She was torn in two by his illness, but instinct told her
immediately that to be his nursemaid was to invite
danger. She had about as much backbone in his presence
as an earthworm. How much worse would she be if she
was to be confronted by a weakened Adam?

And maybe, she thought hopefully, he really wasn't
that ill. Sam might have exaggerated. Besides, Frances
was the candidate for the job. Cool, beautiful, elegant
Frances... I'll bet, Christina thought acidly, that she
could rustle up a bedside manner from underneath all
that blonde glamour if she thought that it would get her
somewhere.

She knocked on the door and an unrecognisable voice
told her to enter.

Christina went in and then stared, dumbfounded, at
the figure stretched out on the bed in front of her. She
felt as though the rug had been pulled out from under
her feet.

'You're ill,' she said, walking towards the bed and peering down at the sallow face looking at her.

'Of course I'm damn well ill.' His voice sounded weak and irritated. 'Didn't Sam tell you?'

'Yes,' Christina admitted reluctantly.

'But you thought otherwise?' He closed his eyes and for a moment panic gripped her. What if he slipped into unconsciousness? He looked ill enough for that.

She hovered uncertainly and his eyes suddenly flew open and some of the old mockery was there.

'Don't worry, I'm not contagious. Not unless the same mosquito that got to me also decided to pay you a visit, which is highly unlikely. So you can sit down and stop standing there as though you're about to be attacked.'

Christina perched uncomfortably on the edge of the bed. She had been full of what she wanted to say, but now she found herself searching around for a gentler way of telling him that she couldn't possibly stay on the island to look after him.

'Sam said that you want me to look after you,' she began, and she could see him reacting already, his face darkening with anger because he could read what she was about to say.

'But...?'

'Adam, I can't take the time off.' She looked at him helplessly, knowing that the real reason was a deep fear of being isolated with him once again. She was far more vulnerable now than she had been when they had gone to the cottage in Scotland. But his appearance was tugging at her, making her want to reach out and comfort him.

'Can't or won't? I'll pay you, of course. You'll be generously reimbursed for the inconvenience.' He closed his eyes again, as though the exertion of his anger had drained him of what little energy he possessed.

His breathing was shallow and irregular and she looked at him in alarm.

'Are you sure that this isn't more serious than you're telling me?' she asked worriedly. 'You look awful. Should I get in touch with Fiona? She'd never forgive me if...if...'

'If something happened to me out here?' He looked at her through his lashes. 'I'm not about to die. So don't you dare phone my sister. You know what she's like. She'll fly over here at the speed of sound and drive me to a premature grave with her worrying.'

Every little burst of speech seemed to weaken him.

'Don't talk,' Christina said soothingly. 'I won't phone her.' She paused, trying to think of how she could tell him that she just couldn't stay and look after him. When he was in perfect health she could hide her love by arguing with him, by stirring herself to feel resentment at his arrogance. Now that he was in this debilitated state, she felt captive to her emotions, without the defences of anger normally open to her.

'Does Frances know about this?' she asked after a while, and he nodded. 'Then,' Christina suggested, looking away, 'perhaps she might like to stay here and take care of you herself.'

'If you can't bring yourself to do this, then fine,' he said angrily, attempting to sit up and then falling back on to the pillows with a groan of frustration, 'but leave Frances out of it. I don't want my life complicated with her fussing around.'

Christina greeted this outburst with coolness. She knew what he was getting at. It was all right for her to look after him because to him she was as sexless as a baked potato, despite his temporary flare of curious interest earlier on. But with Frances it would be different. There would be too much intimacy in that situation, and he wouldn't want that. Not when he was ill.

He was beginning to look flushed and drowsy. He pointed to a bottle of pain-killers on the side-table and she fetched two for him, handing them over with a glass of water.

He swallowed them and she watched him, her heart constricting. She had only ever seen him in command. When, growing up, she and Fiona had succumbed to flu, he had shrugged it off, as though his life was too busy, too full to be inconvenienced by such little things as ill health.

'I'll look after you, Adam,' she heard herself saying. 'I shall have to make a few calls, try and get some of my clients re-scheduled. When are you due to leave here and how?'

'Tomorrow—by taxi,' he said succinctly. 'The hotel can easily arrange a taxi to take me—us—there.' He drew a deep breath and she frowned. 'I suppose Sam's told you that Clive isn't going to be around. He was, in fact, supposed to have left the island last week, but he postponed his duties so that we could meet up.' He looked at her and there was a spark of his old energy in his eyes. 'You don't have to tell me how inconvenient this all is. I never get ill. This is the first time for as long as I can remember and it's bloody frustrating.'

She wanted to smile at that. It was such a typical reaction.

'I must go and see about my packing,' she murmured, pausing by the door before she left. 'Is there someone . . . ?'

'Sam. He's going to stay on the sofa tonight. I feel like a damned invalid,' he muttered with resentment.

'You are a damned invalid,' Christina said drily. 'There's not much point in fighting that.'

He looked as though he heartily disagreed with every word of that pronouncement, but before he could tire himself out with arguing she let herself out of the room and headed back to her own bedroom.

It was only as she was packing her bags that the reality of the situation struck her. For the second time in little more than a month she would find herself cloistered with Adam and out of her depth. It was as if fate was conspiring against her.

She had an early meal with the rest of the crew, who spent the entire time bemoaning their imminent departure and speculating on the weather conditions in England. Frances, she noticed, hardly said a word throughout the meal. She picked at her food, her mouth downturned. After her venomous attack earlier on, Christina half expected her to follow it up with another tirade, but nothing, although those glances, thrown her way ever so often, left her in no doubt that Adam was classified as unfinished business.

But there would be no opportunity to find herself in a position of self-defence. They would all be gone by the time she emerged the following morning, and for that she was heartily grateful.

As promised, the taxi had been arranged, and after a solitary breakfast Christina ventured to Adam's bedroom to see whether he was ready. He was. Just.

His face looked drawn and haggard and there was rough stubble on his cheeks. He looked at her ill-humouredly as she entered the room, and she returned his gaze with sympathy. He hated being ill. If he hadn't already informed her of the fact, she would have guessed it easily enough from the expression on his face.

'Stop feeling sorry for me, dammit,' he muttered, trying to heave himself out of the chair by the window and barely succeeding.

Christina went across to him and offered him her shoulder, which he accepted in bad grace.

'I'm not feeling sorry for you,' she lied, and he gave her a disbelieving glare which she met with equanimity. 'Have you taken any antibiotics? Did the doctor prescribe anything?'

'No, he didn't. Apart, that is, from pain-killers, which I've taken. Liberally.'

She looked at him in alarm. 'I hope not.'

'Oh, for God's sake, don't start subjecting me to your worry.'

He was leaning heavily against her as they made their way out to the reception area. And he was, she knew, resenting every moment of it all.

A porter was dispatched to the bedrooms to fetch their various bits of luggage, and then began the journey to Adam's friend's house.

It wasn't a long journey. Christina allowed her thoughts to drift as she stared out of the window of the air-conditioned car. The crisp, clear blue of the skies, the dazzling reflection of the sun on the foliage, the exuberance of flowers and colour, still hadn't lost its impact for her. She looked with interest at the fruit and vegetable stalls scattered at the side of the road, at the vivid yellows and reds and oranges of the flowers and the different shades of green of the trees, and before she knew it the car was turning left, into what was obviously a well-to-do neighbourhood.

They drove past massive houses, sprawling, imaginatively designed affairs surrounded by immaculately tended gardens. Then, through a security gate, to a row of three-tiered townhouses.

Next to her, Adam had fallen asleep. She looked at him briefly. Despite his illness he was still devilishly handsome, with that dark, tousled hair and the aristocratic set of his features. She had to drag her eyes away before she shook him gently to inform him that they had arrived.

He woke immediately. For a minute she was tempted to believe, to hope, that he had picked up some of his strength, but once they were inside the house he became weary, and looked at her with an expression of angry frustration.

'Don't fight it,' she said gently, helping him up the stairs and into one of the two bedrooms on the first floor. Then she lugged his suitcase into the room and deposited it.

He was sitting on the bed, his elbows resting on his knees. He looked up as she entered and said, 'Well?'

'Well, what?'

'You'll have to give me a hand changing,' he said bluntly, and she felt herself go bright red.

'Surely not,' she stammered. 'Can't you manage?'

'Oh, for God's sake. I wish I could. But I can't, so don't start going coy on me.' He lay down on the bed and she looked at him helplessly. He was right, of course. He was still weak beyond belief and in no state to undress himself.

She walked across and tentatively unbuckled his belt, then began fiddling with the buttons on his shirt, and all the time she could feel her fingers, gauche and trembling.

'I'm not contagious,' he muttered irritably, misreading her expression, and she didn't correct him. Let him think that that was the reason for her appalling state of nerves.

She finally managed to remove his shirt and then she tugged down his trousers, revealing a pair of dark boxer shorts underneath.

No less than she would have seen on a beach, she told herself, but somehow this was different and she was shamelessly fascinated by the length of his muscular legs, the dark hairs on them, the whipcord slimness of his waist and hips.

On their way to the bedroom he had briefly pointed out the air-conditioning system to her, and she went there now to switch it on, feeling instant relief as cool air flooded the place. She needed it. She felt as though she was burning up, on fire.

She returned to the bedroom and was rummaging around in his suitcase for some pyjamas when he said with a trace of amusement in his voice, 'What are you doing?'

'Trying,' Christina said calmly, 'to locate a pair of pyjamas.'

'How solicitous, but don't bother. I never wear the things.'

She dismissed the image that that remark conjured up, and stood next to the bed, her arms folded.

'You can't sleep like that,' she pointed out. 'You've been running a high fever. You need to be clothed.'

'True,' he agreed readily. 'How sensible of you. I suppose that common sense extends to your own wardrobe, or are you going to surprise me by telling me that you sometimes sleep with nothing on?'

'I'm not going to tell you anything at all,' she replied, wondering how it was that he managed to find the strength from somewhere to be mocking.

'Shame,' he murmured, 'the image would have been a wonderful one to fall asleep with.'

Christina ignored that because, if she rose to the bait, then she would start on a round of arguments in which he was in no fit state to indulge.

'Would your friend have some?' she asked, and he nodded drowsily, pointing up to indicate the bedroom on the top floor.

Christina hurried up and managed to locate some. Maybe, she thought, running back down the stairs, he would be asleep on her return to the bedroom. That way he might be a dead weight to manoeuvre into a pair of pyjamas, but then, on the other hand, she would not have to cope with his taunting little remarks.

He was. She breathed a sigh of relief and eased him into the top, hearing his soft, irritated grunts with a mixture of tenderness and impatience. Then she began slipping on the loose-fitting bottoms. She could feel the sexy, abrasive rub of his legs against her hands, and as she pulled the trousers up to his waist a faint hardening beneath her fingers indicated that he was not as deeply asleep as she would have liked.

He had felt the pressure of her hands brushing over his groin, and his body had responded automatically.

Christina averted her eyes, scarlet, and as she did so his blue eyes clashed with hers. He didn't say a word, though. In fact, he looked so utterly serious that she wondered whether he was really aware of what his body had just betrayed, because he promptly shut his eyes and was snoring gently by the time she left the room a few minutes later.

The little incident had shaken her up, though. As she had felt him stirring beneath her, her own body had involuntarily responded by becoming hot and damp, in ready longing for the accidental touch to turn into something deeper.

She began investigating the kitchen, wandering around the small downstairs lounge, staring through the closed patio doors to the small square of land at the back, laid with large terracotta tiles which gave it a charming Italian appearance.

This wasn't going to be easy. She wasn't some kind of nurse, trained to sublimate her emotions underneath a veneer of cold professionalism. By nature, she was not given to outbursts, but her face, she knew, could still betray her. And he knew her too well. He would be able to read behind the slightest glimmer of expression to what lay beneath.

The next three days passed in an agony of trying to disguise her feelings. She hoped that he was too ill to notice the way her hands trembled every time they came into contact with his body, the way her eyes would flit compulsively to his face, drinking in the strong lines, the way that any sudden move or remark from him could make her mouth go dry.

She was so absorbed in her efforts to hide all this that she was hardly aware of his gradual recovery. It registered somewhere that he was on his feet a bit more, that his need for pain-killers was abating, that his colour was returning to normal—all signs that his illness was passing.

She was carrying up a tray of food for him, her usual habit over the past few days, when she was startled to see him emerging from the bathroom, his hair wet from recent washing, a towel casually and, from where she was standing, precariously draped around his waist.

'No need to look like a goldfish,' he commented drily. 'I'm feeling much better this morning.' He followed her into the bedroom and she continued looking at him in alarm.

'Should you be out of bed?' she stammered, depositing the tray on the table next to the bed and hovering indecisively next to it.

'Well, I can't stay there forever.' He turned around and began rooting around for some clothes in the wardrobe. 'I thought that today we might get some fresh air. You must be feeling nearly as claustrophobic as I am.' He extracted a shirt and a pair of trousers from the wardrobe and tossed them past her on to the bed.

'Quite,' Christina said incoherently. 'I mean, now that you're back on your feet, perhaps we should be thinking of the return flight to England?'

He moved towards her and she eyed his damp torso with mounting panic.

'Perhaps we should,' he agreed. 'I want you to know,' he continued slowly, 'that I appreciate what you've done for me. I hate saying this—maybe it's my damned masculine pride—but I couldn't have coped on my own.'

She wished that he would move to another part of the room. She could smell that clean, fresh male scent and it was going to her head like incense.

'It was nothing,' she returned roughly, looking away.

His hand moved to the side of her head, tilting it to face him.

'It was a great deal,' he said softly, 'although it's kind of you to play it down. But then, underneath that cool career-woman veneer you're terribly kind, aren't you?'

'Am I?'

'I think so.' His voice was low and husky and should have warned her of what was to come, but it didn't. The impact of his lips on hers caught her totally by surprise. She tried to pull away—she had all the best intentions in the world of resisting the flood of emotions sweeping through her—but his hold tightened and she closed her eyes with a soft moan.

She felt her hands move to his waist, then slide to stroke his back.

He eased her on to the bed, still kissing her, and then unhurriedly unbuttoned her blouse.

She could have stopped him. He wasn't overpowering her. But something in her had finally broken. Maybe all those days of caring for him, of surreptitiously feeding her love on the sight of him, had caught up with her. All she knew was that she wanted him, whatever the consequences.

He pushed aside the thin material and began caressing her breasts, playing with them in the same leisurely way that he was kissing her, as if they had all the time in the world, teasing the nipples into hard arousal.

'You're ill,' she moaned weakly, and he said against her mouth,

'I've never felt better, believe me.' Then his lips burnt a path along her neck, moving to suck her breasts, first one then the other, flicking his tongue over the nipples until she wanted to cry out with desire.

She gripped his head, her fingers tangling in his dark hair, and urged him to caress her harder, while she writhed under his exploring mouth.

His towel had been discarded at some point, and she could feel him, hard and wanting against her body. It was unbearably erotic.

Her shorts were disposed of quickly, followed by her underwear, and she parted her legs to his hand, squirming as he sought and found her most intimate areas.

She felt as though she were going mad. She wanted him so much.

He licked her stomach, then moved lower until she gasped with shock and pleasure as his tongue followed where his fingers had shortly before been.

He grasped her thighs with either hand, and she writhed against him, giving soft, low moans of pure ecstasy.

When he finally thrust into her, her whole world exploded, and she realised two things in a blinding flash.

The first was that no man had ever, nor could ever, arouse her as this man could. And the second was that she would sleep with him for as long as he wanted her, even though deep inside the pain of being rejected was already starting to hurt.

'I knew it,' he said later, lazily, stroking her stomach with the flat of his hand. 'I wanted to be your first lover, and I was. Greg meant nothing to you, did he?'

Christina turned away and shrugged. He made it sound so casual; he was so *pleased* that she had not slept with anyone before him. In a way she hated him for that and hated herself for putting the final nail in her coffin. Now there was nothing left of her; she had given it all to him, every last piece of her, including her virginity. It was a frightening thought and one which she viewed dispassionately. No point moaning and groaning and regretting. He already had her love, so what was the small addition of her body?

He was talking to her, softly, stroking her until her body quivered under his touch and she parted her legs, opening herself up to him, and as she closed her eyes she saw the pleasure on his face. Not love, but pleasure, and she tried not to remember that pleasure was short-lived.

CHAPTER TEN

'I'M PREGNANT.'

There was a look of triumph on her face as she said this. Outside it was raining, a bleak grey persistent drizzle, one of those wintry downpours that made you want to curl up underneath a blanket and hibernate for a couple of months.

Christina heard the soft patter like a sudden thunderstorm, drumming in her head until she wanted to faint. She wanted badly to say something, but her mouth felt as dry as ashes. She looked at Frances, framed in the doorway, thin as a reed in an ivory-coloured coat that swept down almost to her ankles and was tightly belted at the waist, and couldn't find a thing to say.

'Well, aren't you going to invite me in?' Frances stepped into the room without waiting for an answer to that one and swung around, her eyebrows arched as she took in the modesty of the décor.

Christina shut the door, very quietly. She wanted to do everything very quietly, because any sudden movement and she knew that her head would burst.

Why did this come as such a shock to her? she wondered. Had she really thought that Adam was going to rip away the barriers he had erected against committing himself to a woman and plead for her on bended knee? Not likely. In which case, why did Frances's declaration make her want to collapse in horror? It wasn't as though she had any prior claim on Adam Palmer. She had known that he was no celibate. Had she seriously expected him to curtail his sexual life because of her?

They had spent five days together in Trinidad, five blindingly wonderful days. They had talked and explored and made love and she had convinced herself that in that land of fairy-tales nothing could go wrong.

But things did go wrong, didn't they, in real life? Even before they'd arrived back to the dismal reality of English soil, she had already begun to feel the first qualms about their relationship. In the heat of the tropical sunshine it had seemed unassailable, but by the time they had stepped on to the plane bound for Heathrow it was all beginning to feel like a holiday romance—a period of passion followed by a blast of reality, then all the expected withdrawal symptoms.

What made it worse was that she knew Adam. She knew that his world did not revolve around commitment to one quite plain, physically nondescript photographer. He might have taken her into his bed, a combination of gratitude and a lazy, amused acceptance of her willingness to sleep with him, but as soon as they had taken off from the airport reality had reasserted itself with frightening speed.

They had parted from each other at Heathrow in a flurry of haste and confusion. A chauffeur had been sent for Adam. There was some crisis at the company and his presence was urgently required at a meeting. He had shot her a regretful look and she could see that he was already retreating.

'I'll be in touch,' he had thrown over his shoulder, as he hurried behind the chauffeur and was absorbed by the milling crowds. She had barely had the time to acknowledge his departure.

She had caught a taxi back to her flat and all the way she had replayed in her mind, in agonising slow motion, the indifferent casualness of his parting. No bursts of emotion, no dinner date arranged. They could have been strangers.

That was one week ago, Or rather, six days, five hours and a handful of minutes.

Frances was browsing around the room, eyeing this and that, elegant fingers trailing over the bookshelf, along the spines of the books, before coming to rest on the mantelpiece, which was the one striking feature in the flat. She turned to face Christina and her eyes were glittering with victory.

'I said that he was meant for me,' Christina heard her say, from some very great distance, through a haze of confused pain, 'and I meant it. Every word. Did you think that you could net him by sleeping with him? Did you think that you had that much to offer in between the sheets?'

'How pregnant are you? You don't look pregnant.'

That brought a frown of anger to Frances's perfect features. 'I'm only a couple of months. Nothing will be showing.' The complacent look returned. 'If you have any pride, you'll leave him alone now. You must know that Adam would never abandon a lady in distress.'

Frances fluttered her eyelashes with a pretence of helplessness and Christina balled her fists in sudden rage.

'I had no intention of continuing what was started over there,' she managed to mutter through clenched teeth. 'So you and your threats can get the hell out of my flat. Now!'

'I suppose that means that you've realised that you don't have a hope in hell of marrying him?'

'Out! Now!'

Frances began retreating as Christina moved towards her. The pounding in her ears was getting stronger and stronger, threatening to take over completely.

'Leave him alone!' Frances said, as her mask of smug control slipped to reveal the angry, hissing animal underneath.

'You're welcome to him!' Christina retorted, her whole body trembling as if she was in deep shock. 'I have more sense than to ever let myself get involved with him! I feel sorry for you if you're prepared to go to such lengths to trap him into a loveless marriage! You give women a bad name!'

Frances's porcelain face was rigid with anger. They stared at each other, and Christina thought hysterically, What a snapshot for the photo album. Me, watching my life crumble away, and her, blonde and beautiful and wicked beyond words. Then the moment disintegrated as Frances turned on her heel and walked quickly out of the flat, slamming the door behind her.

Christina sat on the sofa, her head in her hands, and for the first time since she had returned to England allowed herself to cry, long, racking sobs that felt as though they would tear her apart. She had no idea how long she had sat there, but when she finally did stand up her limbs were numb and aching and it was dark outside.

So another chapter of my life has just ebbed past, she thought, and I felt as though I had learnt something from Greg, which just goes to show that a fool will always be a fool. She tried to be philosophical, to tell herself that Frances's declaration didn't change the fact that Adam had been toying with her in Trinidad, that she had been nothing more than a little diversion, but she just couldn't surmount the image of Frances, carrying *his* child. She, Christina, had made sure, making lazy love with Adam, that there was no way that she could fall pregnant, but now she wished desperately that she hadn't been so conscientious. Not that she would have ever told him, far less used it as a lever to trap him into marriage. No, she would have just loved to be carrying his baby, to know that something wonderful and positive had emerged from her fruitless love.

Three days later, when Adam finally phoned, apologising for not having contacted her sooner and blaming it on an overseas emergency, she was ready for him.

Her heart was still beating hard, though, as she said coldly, 'Forget about the apologies, Adam. I'm surprised you saw fit to call at all.'

'I told you,' he repeated curtly. 'I was abroad. Anyway, I needed time to think.'

'What about? Not us, I hope, because as far as I'm concerned I won't be wasting much sleep on that.' She wasn't going to give him the satisfaction of thinking that he had hooked her, but every word was breaking her heart.

'And what the hell is that supposed to mean? I——'

'What do you think it means?' Christina cut in acidly. 'I don't want anything to do with you, and I don't want you to call this number again—if it was your intention to do so, though, knowing you, that's open to debate.'

'Dammit, Tina——!'

'Or maybe I'm wrong,' she said, closing her eyes and clenching her fingers so tightly around the telephone cord that her nails bit into her palm. 'Maybe it's your style to sleep around even when your ex-lover is pregnant with your child.'

If she had knocked him unconscious she couldn't have silenced him more effectively. Now, she thought, now would be the perfect moment to hang up, but she didn't.

'That's impossible. Now would you like to explain that?' he asked tightly.

'Impossible? Ha! And I would have thought that it was self-explanatory. In fact I'm surprised that she hasn't told you herself already.'

'As I said, I've been out of the country. I've only just this minute stepped foot back in the house, and I don't have a clue what the hell you're talking about.'

Christina licked her lips. 'I think I'll leave the explanations for Frances,' she said.

'Why? You've already done one hell of a job of ruining my return, and anyway, if you'd like to just listen for a minute——'

'No, I would not!' she said with rising anger. What, she thought, do you think you've managed to do with my *life*? 'I should go and have a bath, then have a drink, then sit down to wait for her arrival.'

'Now you listen to me——!'

'No,' she yelled into the receiver, '*you* listen to *me*! I don't want anything further to do with you! Sleeping with you was the biggest mistake I ever had the misfortune to make and I don't intend to compound it by ever setting eyes on you again! Do you hear me?'

'Loud,' his voice reached her, 'and bloody clear.' And he denied her the final luxury of hanging up by doing so himself, leaving her to cradle the receiver until she felt as though her fingers had become welded to it.

I won't die because of this, she told herself the following day as she tried to make herself resume the reins of her life. Nobody ever died of a broken heart. But the agony followed her every movement and thoughts of him dogged her every step until by the end of the day she wanted to scream in pain and frustration. She had no idea how to cope with it. Greg's departure from her life was, in comparison to what she was feeling now, a picnic, but then she had never been in love with him, had she?

Over the next week, nothing got better. How could she find a way out? she wondered desperately. She tried to summon up enthusiasm in her work, to drown herself in it, but her lack of concentration wouldn't let her. The only thing she could focus on was Adam—Adam and Frances—and thoughts of them revolved around and around until she felt as though she was going crazy.

She was sitting, staring blankly at the television screen, trying not to think of the long, empty days stretching out in front of her, years which Adam had rendered devoid of any meaning, when there was a knocking on the door. Or rather something more like a hammering. It was a noise that demanded answering, and Christina clicked her tongue impatiently. Her neighbours had been acting up recently. They were both art students, each with an enormous capacity for generous displays of temperament, and over the past few days she had been subjected to their various tirades. They had been in the flats almost as long as she had, and they used her as their sounding-board.

Usually Christina was very patient with their temper tantrums, but right now she was in no mood for yet another ear bending. She was going through her own personal catastrophe and she didn't have the patience at eleven o'clock in the night to deal with other people's arguments.

So she yanked open the door, but instead of a petulant Arthur or an angry Yolande she was faced with Adam's remarkable face, and he didn't give her time to withdraw either. He pushed open the door, pushing her backwards with it, walking into her flat as though he had every right to be there.

Christina's mind struggled to grapple with the enormity of seeing him there, in her flat, after she had spent what seemed like a lifetime conjuring up his image. She might have guessed that he was taller, harder, more aggressively handsome than she had remembered.

He had divested himself of his jacket by tossing it on one of the chairs and he rolled up the sleeves of his shirt, exposing his muscled forearms, sprinkled with dark hairs.

Christina watched all this in fascination. She couldn't take her eyes off him, but slowly her brain got back into gear and she rounded on him with a surge of fury.

'What are you doing here?' Being near him was like a starving man being near to a plate of food, only able to watch and yearn and remember how good it once was to eat, and that vulnerability made her even angrier with him.

'I don't want you here!' she shouted, walking across to the door and yanking it open.

'Shut that door!' he ordered, moving swiftly towards her, but she held her ground, until he slammed shut the door and picked her up bodily, ignoring her frantic struggles.

'What,' she panted, 'do you think you're doing?'

'What I've wanted to do for the longest while, which is——' he dumped her unceremoniously on to the sofa and pinned her arms to her sides so that she couldn't move '—to sit you down and make you listen to what I have to say.'

'I don't want to hear what you've got to say, Adam, and anyway, it doesn't matter. You have someone else to think of apart from yourself.'

'What are you talking about?' he asked after a pause, bewildered.

Christina risked a look at that dark face and felt faint.

'Your child?' she reminded him bitterly.

She didn't know what she expected him to do in response to that, but the one thing she didn't expect was for him to laugh.

'You might see the funny side——' she began, spitting hostility.

'You witch,' he murmured, as his laughter subsided. He fixed her with his amazing blue eyes and her heart flipped over. He absent-mindedly stroked her wrist with his thumb and that little inconsequential gesture brought the blood rushing to her head.

'I——'

'Shut up,' he said calmly, 'and listen to me.'

'I don't have much choice, do I? With my ha——'

'I said shut up.'

She gave him an impotent glare which he met with an amused look, then he said bluntly, 'About Frances.'

She felt her body tense, and she had to force herself to breathe normally, not to let him see how much she was hurting. She had no idea what he was doing here, but, if it was to rekindle a bit of temporary passion, then she wasn't having it. And if it was to talk about Frances, then she wasn't having that either. She just wanted to be left alone with her misery. Couldn't he see that? He didn't owe her any explanations.

'There's no need to explain about Frances,' she said tightly. 'You don't owe me anything.'

'Don't I?' he murmured, his voice a lazy caress that sent an unwelcome shiver through her. 'After your revelation, I paid Frances a little visit.'

'So you know what I'm talking about,' Christina said in a dull voice.

'Oh, I know exactly what you're talking about, but you're way off target. I told you when you spoke to me that the whole thing was impossible, but you weren't about to listen, were you?'

Christina had switched off by this point. Her mind had gone off on a different tangent from the minute she'd begun to believe that Frances might not have been pregnant after all. Although why would she lie?

'Why should I?' she said, trying to show disinterest, because did it matter whether he was involved with Frances or not? The fact was that he would never be involved with *her* and she would never settle for anything but the whole works—marriage, children, the lot. Not for her a temporary dalliance with him.

'You witch.' He gave her a slow smile and she licked her lips in confused apprehension.

'Stop calling me that,' she muttered, lowering her eyes.

'Why? Is it too close to the truth for your liking? But back to Frances. I went round to see her because I was intrigued by what you had said.'

'Why? I thought you were harbouring thoughts of marrying her. I would have thought you'd be delighted.'

'Don't interrupt.'

'Don't tell me not to...'

He didn't answer. Instead he stroked her face with such unexpected tenderness that she was immediately rendered mute.

'That's more like it,' he murmured. 'Now are you about to let me finish what I have to say? I confronted Frances because there was no way that she could be pregnant, at least not by me, and, knowing her, not by anyone, but flying round to your flat with that lie was so immensely vengeful that I couldn't let her off without airing my views on the matter. I wanted to see her wriggle like a worm on a hook, and by God she did. What kind of man do you think I am? How could you have thought that I would sleep with another woman when I was already under your spell?'

Christina could picture the scene. Adam would have had her in a state of total disarray. He would have given her hell.

'Why would she lie?' she asked, too scared to believe what her heart was telling her.

'Why do you think? "Hell hath no fury", as the saying goes. She couldn't have me and she knew it, but she wasn't going to let you have me either. She has quite an optimistic image of herself. She feels that she's irresistible to all men, and the fact that I wasn't about to join the procession was too much for her to bear. She had set her sights on me and there was no way that she was going to relinquish her potential conquest because of you. I shan't tell you what she had to say about the whole thing. Most of it's unrepeatable.'

'Poor woman,' Christina murmured bitterly. 'Any fool can see that you're not the marrying kind.'

'Could you?' he asked softly.

'Of course, and that was before you told me about your parents.' She began to fiddle, twisting her fingers together. 'Look,' she said, meeting those amazing blue eyes steadily, even though her heart was doing very odd things in her chest, 'I don't really know why you told me about Frances, but there was no need. What we had is over and done with and I'm quite happy to accept that.'

'Why?'

'Why what?' she asked blankly.

'Are you so happy to accept it, when you're head over heels in love with me?'

There was a dreadful silence, during which she felt herself dying a thousand deaths. She couldn't even croak out a denial, not when he was staring at her like that, as though he could see into her head, into her soul.

'Because you are, aren't you?'

She felt the prick of tears behind her eyes. 'More fool me,' she whispered. 'You'd think that I'd have learnt something after Greg. As you were so eager to inform me, he was hardly a shining example of moral rectitude.' She laughed, a bitter sound. 'And you, of all people.'

'As if you hadn't learnt from the last time, all those
years ago, when you made the colossal mistake of developing a crush on me.'

'Please don't laugh.'

'I'm not laughing,' he said in a low voice. He tilted
her chin so that she was looking at him, right into his
eyes. 'I was a fool all those years ago. I should have
grabbed out to you and made sure that you never got
away, because you made me feel special then, and you're
the only woman who's ever succeeded in doing that.
When we found ourselves marooned in that cottage I
felt as though, in some strange way, I'd come home.'

Christina was hardly breathing. If she was imagining
all this, if she was crazy, then she never wanted sanity
to return.

'What are you saying?' she asked.

'I'm saying, as if it weren't obvious, that I'm nuts
about you—mad, insane, call it what you will, but I love
you to death.'

'You do?' Now this surely was a dream, but it wasn't.
She knew that when he lowered his head and his mouth
brushed against her, lightly and persuasively, tantalising
foreplay.

'If you thought that you wanted to make sure, after
Greg, that your fingers were never burnt again, then
you'd better believe that I felt even more so. Do you
know, you're the only person in whom I've ever confided the state of my parents' marriage? That's when I
knew that something odd was going on, that you were
weaving some kind of spell over me, and it was frightening. Nothing had prepared me for falling in love.
Making money, yes, I knew all about that, just as I knew
all about making love, but what I felt for you was like
a bolt from the blue. I suddenly found myself wishing
that I had got to know you—I mean really know you—

much sooner, but our paths never seemed to cross, did they?'

'Only in passing,' Christina admitted, in a daze. She gasped as his hand travelled downwards to her breast, cupping it until it swelled in agonising response.

'Why? I wonder.'

'We moved in different circles,' she said, her breath catching in her throat as his fingers began to play with her nipple, rubbing it gently, hypnotically, through her top. 'I can't think properly when you do that,' she said unevenly, and he smiled.

'Good. I suppose,' he continued thoughtfully, reaching under her jumper to stroke her stomach, before gently unzipping her trousers, 'I suppose you're right. I only ever seemed to see you in the company of Fiona, when there were millions of other people milling about, at some wretched social gathering. I can remember countless Christmas parties when I could just about glimpse you in between the thousands. I always got the impression that you were avoiding me.'

'Did you?' Christina asked lazily, enjoying what his exploring hand was doing to her, and enjoying what he was saying even more. 'I wonder why.'

'Could it have anything to do with the fact that all I ever seemed to get out of you was a polite little wave, a polite little smile, occasionally a bit of small talk, then a quick look around before you made your escape?'

'Can you blame me?' she asked, smiling. 'I was at a very impressionable age when you made it clear that my teenage crush was something of a joke.'

'So you spent the next eight years or so avoiding me?'

'Not actually avoiding.'

'Well, you'll have to get used to me being around from now on, because I won't be letting you run away again.'

'And how do you propose to do that?' she teased, liking the unusual feeling of power over him.

'By putting a certain little gold band around your finger, and if necessary I'll even resort to begging.'

'Is that a marriage proposal, Adam Palmer?' she asked breathlessly.

'I take it you'll do me the honour?'

She didn't have to answer that one. The reply was in her eyes and he smiled at her.

'I wonder what Fiona will say?' she mused after a while, when the delicious prospect of being married to him was beginning to sink in.

'I should think, knowing my sister, that after two seconds of surprise she'll accept it as if it were the most expected thing in the world. Not that she'll have much time to devote to us. She's head over heels in love, so she informs me, with my highly suitable blind date.'

He laughed and she had to chuckle at the devilish gleam in his eyes. 'I guess you think you know everything, don't you?' Christina asked wryly, and he shot her a lingering look from under his lashes.

'I knew you loved me. Not immediately, but gradually it began to dawn on me, somewhere in my subconscious. When I went out to Trinidad it was half to follow you and half to try and see whether the presence of Frances might put what I was feeling for you into perspective. You see, I really didn't want my life complicated by falling in love—not that I considered that an option for me anyway. But you managed to get under my skin and I found that I was powerless to do anything about it.'

'Powerless?' she asked with mock-incredulity.

'Who would have thought it? When we got back to England, I'd made up my mind that the whole thing was ridiculous, that love was not something I believed in, that I was far too cynical to be caught in that particular trap, that if I stayed away from you long enough things would return to normal. But that was just wishful thinking. I tried and I failed.'

'Good.' She guided his hand to her breast, covering it with her own as he massaged it with slow, sensuous movements. 'It's nice to know that you're not completely failure-proof.'

He gave her a smouldering look that brought a heady flush to her cheeks. 'I'm glad you like the thought of that,' he murmured silkily. 'Now perhaps you'd like to shut up? There are better things to do than talk.' His head dipped and she felt his mouth circle her nipple, alternately sucking and licking until she groaned for him to satisfy her.

'I've waited a long time for this, woman,' he said huskily. 'I'm going to take my time; I want to enjoy every bit of you.'

His tongue trailed a path along her stomach and she felt his hands expertly loosening her clothes until she was naked and erotically turned on by his intense appreciation of her body.

He moved down to part her thighs and she surrendered to his exploration with a moan of contentment, squirming when that exploration became exquisite agony. Only then did he remove his own clothes, to resume the teasing, sensual exploration, while he guided her hand to him.

'Oh, God,' she whispered huskily, when his tongue, flicking over her, was proving too tormenting, and he half smiled, as feverish now for fulfilment as she was.

She was a flower opening for him, and as he thrust into her she arched back in deep excitement.

Later, lying together, with her head cradled against his shoulder, he said unsteadily, 'Now that you've managed to make an honest man out of me, I might as well warn you that I want nothing short of the whole hog.'

'Mmm?' she whispered languidly, kissing his neck and loving the way she could feel his arousal at that small, feathery caress.

'Mmm,' he said lazily, 'the whole hog—children, the lot.'

'I might,' Christina sighed happily, 'just decide to oblige you in that.'

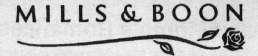

MILLS & BOON

Forthcoming Titles

DUET
Available in April

The Betty Neels Duet   **A SUITABLE MATCH**
THE MOST MARVELLOUS SUMMER

The Emma Darcy Duet   **PATTERN OF DECEIT**
BRIDE OF DIAMONDS

FAVOURITES
Available in April

NOT WITHOUT LOVE Roberta Leigh
NIGHT OF ERROR Kay Thorpe

LOVE ON CALL
Available in April

VET IN A QUANDARY Mary Bowring
NO SHADOW OF DOUBT Abigail Gordon
PRIORITY CARE Mary Hawkins
TO LOVE AGAIN Laura MacDonald

Next Month's Romances

Each month you can choose from a wide variety of romance with Mills & Boon. Below are the new titles to look out for next month, why not ask either Mills & Boon Reader Service or your Newsagent to reserve you a copy of the titles you want to buy — just tick the titles you would like and either post to Reader Service or take it to any Newsagent and ask them to order your books.

Please save me the following titles:		Please tick	✓
AN UNSUITABLE WIFE	Lindsay Armstrong		
A VENGEFUL PASSION	Lynne Graham		
FRENCH LEAVE	Penny Jordan		
PASSIONATE SCANDAL	Michelle Reid		
LOVE'S PRISONER	Elizabeth Oldfield		
NO PROMISE OF LOVE	Lilian Peake		
DARK MIRROR	Daphne Clair		
ONE MAN, ONE LOVE	Natalie Fox		
LOVE'S LABYRINTH	Jessica Hart		
STRAW ON THE WIND	Elizabeth Power		
THE WINTER KING	Amanda Carpenter		
ADAM'S ANGEL	Lee Wilkinson		
RAINBOW ROUND THE MOON	Stephanie Wyatt		
DEAR ENEMY	Alison York		
LORD OF THE GLEN	Frances Lloyd		
OLD SCHOOL TIES	Leigh Michaels		

If you would like to order these books in addition to your regular subscription from Mills & Boon Reader Service please send £1.90 per title to: Mills & Boon Reader Service, Freepost, P.O. Box 236, Croydon, Surrey, CR9 9EL, quote your Subscriber No:.................................. (If applicable) and complete the name and address details below. Alternatively, these books are available from many local Newsagents including W H Smith, J Menzies, Martins and other paperback stockists from 8 April 1994.

Name:...

Address:...

....Post Code:...........................

To Retailer: If you would like to stock M&B books please contact your regular book/magazine wholesaler for details.

You may be mailed with offers from other reputable companies as a result of this application. If you would rather not take advantage of these opportunities please tick box ☐